A WAY THROUGH THE WOODS

A WAY THROUGH THE WOODS

Katharine McMahon

SINCLAIR-STEVENSON

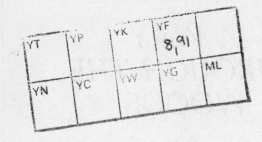

First published in Great Britain by
Sinclair-Stevenson Limited
7/8 Kendrick Mews
London SW7 3HG, England

British Library Cataloguing in Publication Data
A CIP catalogue record for this book is available from the British Library.
ISBN: 1 85619 036 6

Typeset by Colset (Private) Ltd, Singapore
Printed and bound in England by Clays Ltd, St Ives plc

for
MARTIN

They shut the road through the woods
Seventy years ago.
Weather and rain have undone it again,
And now you would never know
There was once a road through the woods
Before they planted the trees.

It is underneath the coppice and heath,
And the thin anemones.
Only the keeper sees
That, where the ring-dove broods,
And the badgers roll at ease,
There was once a way through the woods.

Yet, if you enter the woods
Of a summer evening late,
When the night air cools on the trout-ringed pools
Where the otter whistles his mate,
(They fear not men in the woods,
Because they see so few)
You will hear the beat of a horse's feet,
And the swish of a skirt in the dew,
Steadily cantering through
The misty solitudes,
As though they perfectly knew
The old lost road through the woods ...
But there is no road through the woods!

The Way Through the Woods
Rudyard Kipling

1

JOHN GRESHAM WAS shown into a joyless drawing-room.

No fire burned in the grate, not a speck of dust softened the polished bureau or chair legs, even the late spring flowers stood meekly to attention in symmetrical arrays of pink and white. A blend of gold, cream and subdued green, the room gave no indication that the mistress of the house was a young woman, unless perhaps by the translucent gleam of immaculate, over-elaborate lace curtains. Near the plain mantel was a small inlaid table, its purpose to support two photographs. One must be of Nicholas; the face beneath the uniform cap displayed anonymous, clear-cut features in half profile. The second, oblong mounted, was presumably Sophia, though she was scarcely recognisable to John Gresham; her face looked thin under hair swept back according to pre-war fashion, her gaze remote, her mouth softened only by vaseline on the kind camera lens.

Hearing footsteps, he gently replaced the portrait and turned to the door, and there she was, rather less delicate-featured than in the photograph, very pale, her eyes puzzled but revealing the correct degree of welcome.

"Mr Gresham. What a pleasant surprise."

"I'm sorry to have disturbed you. I wanted to come in person."

She offered him tea, but no, he would not stay, he had just been passing and had an appointment later.

"First, let me congratulate you on your engagement," he said. "I read the announcement, and of course your aunt was very full of it."

She smiled self-consciously and clasped her hands to conceal the ring.

"But I'm afraid it's as the executor of my wife's Will that I've come. She died, you know, in March."

Her poise was fractured, she looked genuinely upset.

"Mrs Gresham! I had no idea. Oh I'm so sorry."

"Yes, well, she had been very ill for a long time, as you were perhaps aware."

"No, I didn't realise. I'm sorry. I'm rather out of touch with my aunt, you see."

"The fact is my wife left you something and I thought. . . . as it might seem. . . . Well, I had other business in town so I thought I'd come."

She was regarding him now with some warmth. She smiled again. "Really I hardly knew her. I can't think why she should leave me anything."

"Oh, it's very small, terribly small, just a couple of notebooks — they were Helen's. I know, it's very odd, but my wife particularly wanted you to have them. She only made the Will in February, you see, and was still very much in her right mind. I couldn't refuse her."

"But how extraordinary! What about Helen? Doesn't she want them?"

"No, no. I checked with her. I wrote. She replied that my wife had discussed it with her. Really she would rather they were thrown away, she said, but she thought it was up to my wife as she'd had them for years. Helen gave them to my wife a long time ago, you see. Helen didn't want them, and Eleanor asked for them."

Sophia's posture had altered. She was leaning forward a little in her chair, her hands clenched together.

"Well, it was really very kind of you to have come all this way to bring them to me."

"No, I was in town. But I haven't brought them. That was the other thing — you have to collect them in person. I'm sorry. They're in Needlewick. It's silly, I know. I would understand if you didn't bother. I'll put them away, or burn them if you'd rather."

Sophia now collapsed back, laughing.

"Really, it's most peculiar. What a mystery! Well, Mr Gresham, I'm afraid I can't say that I've any plans to come to Needlewick at the moment. Colin and I intend to marry in September, you see. Quite soon. There's lots to be done."

"Of course, of course."

He was drawing his feet together, ready for departure. They both stood.

"I'll let you know what I decide, shall I?" she asked, leading him into the hall and opening the front door for him.

"Yes, yes, there's no hurry."

She shook his hand.

"It really was very kind of you to come."

"Not at all, not at all."

Sophia watched Mr Gresham walk hurriedly away, a slight figure, much too frail. She had scarcely known him before; he had been only a tentative, masculine presence, yet his smile now seemed welcome and familiar to her. Poor Mr Gresham, alone.

She closed the heavy door and stood for a moment

smoothing her dress and hair. The visit had left her in a state of nervous excitement. Mrs Gresham was dead.

Upstairs, Sophia stood at a mirror, arrested by her own reflection with its suddenly flushed cheeks. She could picture Eleanor Gresham in her garden, the lawn ripe at her feet, a breeze stirring the brim of her broad hat and the ruffles of her gown.

Sophia turned abruptly from the glass and, though it was far too early, began to dress for dinner. Colin was expected and it was worth taking considerable trouble for him as he always noticed what she wore — his delight in her was perhaps what she most liked about him. It was a pity that, as the hours ticked by, she would become oppressed and irritated by the combined company of Colin and her father. Neither could be natural with the other; it annoyed her particularly that her father's behaviour should be so pleased and deferential. She must insist on going out for a walk with Colin after dinner, although that would mean kisses: hand kisses, cheek kisses she liked; mouth kisses seemed intrusive and a little dirty. It was as if they were being performed under the approving eye of her father even when he was miles away.

Carefully reknotting her hair, she speculated on the contents of Mrs Gresham's Will. "The woman didn't even like me," she would later tell Colin — she mentally rehearsed the words. "She thought I was bad for Helen, I could tell. Haven't I told you about my cousin, Helen Callwood? I went to stay with her when I was about thirteen and Nicholas had measles. It was thought I'd be safer away from the germs and they sent me to stay with my mother's sister, Aunt Margaret, and her husband, who's a doctor, and my cousin, in this tiny village called Needlewick. It's really remote."

That was the summer. That was the summer.

No meal in the presence of Mr Simon Theobald could be comfortable; even Sophia who had dined alone with her father for a number of years could never be at ease, and poor Colin compensated for his anxiety with over-zealous attempts at conversation, clumsy clashing of cutlery and conscientious lip-wiping.

There were elements in Simon Theobald's domestic life which he had failed to control and, as if in compensation, he now clung ever more assiduously to the rituals learnt in childhood. Food must be perfectly served; neither he nor Sophia was permitted to speak without first laying down knife and fork and resting hands on lap; no drop of wine or gravy must splash on the white cloth. At the end of a course Theobald would cleanse imaginary crumbs from his fingers by flicking his thumbs across them several times. Sophia was acutely aware of her father's every indrawn breath and click of teeth. The sight of a soft pudding caused her jaw muscles to clench in anticipation of the unnecessary grinding of his molars through the unresisting blancmange. For her, company at dinner was a blissful release. Colin's proposal, so acceptable to her father, also released her from the torture of meal times; she ceased to be the unwilling focus of all her father's attention and might even laugh or blow her nose.

"Mr Gresham called today, father."

His mouth was full of lamb and young peas. In the time it took him to prepare for speech she had begun to regret this rash revelation.

"Mr Gresham?"

His clear blue gaze, from eyes remarkably large and lavishly lashed, met hers in polite interest.

"Yes. Sorry, I thought you'd know him. He's a lawyer

in Needlewick. I met him when I went to stay there. His wife was a great friend of mother's."

"I know who Mr Gresham is."

"Where's Needlewick?" Colin interrupted.

Now that the Pandora's Box was opened Sophia would have given much to have it closed again. No good would come of it. Already her father's neat movements of knife and fork had become yet more deliberate.

She vented her anger on Colin. "You wouldn't have heard of it, it's a minute village where my mother was born."

"Ah." Colin shot a hurried glance at his host and reached for the dish of potatoes — a spoon bounced on the cloth and flicked spots of melted butter on to the salt cellar.

"Yes, I stayed there once with my aunt and uncle. The Greshams were family friends. It seems that Mrs Gresham has left some books for me. She died. Did you know that, father?"

"I believe it was mentioned."

"But how exciting! Are they of any value, these books?"

"No, I shouldn't think so. Why didn't you tell me Mrs Gresham was dead, father?"

There was another long pause while he completed his meal and pushed his plate a fraction of an inch away. "I had no idea you would be interested. You've never mentioned her."

"She was mama's dearest friend."

"I don't remember your mother ever writing to her much."

"No. No."

Colin came crashing to the rescue. "Talking of writing — I've been defending a fearfully interesting case today. Fraud. Incredible the lengths people will go to . . ."

*

They walked along the Embankment, the wind tossing litter and flying blossom about their ankles. Sophia was soon shivering.

"It's so cold for May."

He drew her closer by tucking her arm through his. "You're not wearing enough. You never do."

"I wanted to get out quickly. Good God, Colin, I don't know how you can bear the atmosphere in that house. You must be mad to inflict it on yourself."

"I'd do far worse for you, Sophia."

"I know you would. I know."

"I sometimes wonder why you deliberately provoke him by talking about your mother."

"I don't do it to provoke him — not entirely. Colin, she's my mother! I have to keep her alive for myself, I do precious little else for her."

"Has she written lately?"

When they talked about her mother, she always felt that his compassionate tone would be more suitable if he was addressing someone dangerously ill or recently bereaved. She despised him for it.

"You know she doesn't write. Why should she, I never write to her." Her raised voice alerted the interest of other strollers and he hurriedly withdrew his arm. "I think my mother will be sorry to know Eleanor Gresham is dead. I wish I'd known her better. I can't think why she thought of me when she was writing her Will."

Overhead cherry blossom hung in dim clusters. Mrs Gresham. The cow parsley in the bank outside her house, her garden hazed by yellow heat and the roses full-blown.

At breakfast two days later Sophia received the letter confirming her unusual legacy. She pushed the envelope to one side and began to spread butter on her toast.

"You received the letter from Gresham, then?"

"Yes."

The morning sunlight through the long voile curtains of the breakfast room was blinding, she had to shield her face.

"Yes, it's absurd. I can't go all the way to Needlewick for such a silly thing. I've far too much to do."

"Although, as I've said, Sophia, you ought to visit your uncle and aunt before your marriage."

"Oh perhaps I might go later in the summer."

"Yes. And you could collect your book then."

Simon Theobald had in part made his fortune by never turning down a gift or an opportunity.

"Maybe, yes."

But later, when her father had left the house, she raged about the rooms in a ferment of emotional energy. What did Helen's diary contain that could be of relevance now? Why had it been given to Eleanor Gresham? And why must Sophia now go to Needlewick when Mr Gresham might so easily have posted it or indeed delivered it himself? Mrs Gresham had undoubtedly become eccentric in the late stages of her illness.

But curiosity burned; Sophia must read the diary which would of course contain many references to her own visit in that summer of 1909. And Needlewick was not after all so very far away; she need only stay overnight or Colin could even motor her up in a day. But she did not want Colin in Needlewick. The thought brought her up short before a large oval mirror on the landing as if suddenly caught rehearsing the name of a secret lover. She did not want Colin in Needlewick.

Finally, for peace, she opened the door of her brother's room.

She recoiled, as always, from the reality of his complete absence. The shutters were closed and in the grey light from the doorway the room was dim, cold and very tidy, for though not kept as a shrine it was unused.

She closed the door, went to the bed and laid her head on the pillow. Nicholas, I wrote to you so often in the Needlewick summer. Do you remember how homesick I was — how you-sick? I would have caught your measles willingly rather than be exiled like that.

She stood up and whispered fiercely: "I'll go, I'll go."

It would be her last trip anywhere without Colin for some time, and she'd tell him that for sentimental reasons she must make it alone. Anyway, he wouldn't be interested in girlish memories.

"I'll go then, shall I, Nicholas? Shall I go?"

Her words fell on the dark carpet, the long bookshelves and the smooth quilt, where they died softly with no ears to hear them.

2

Mrs DEBORAH PARDITER, now widowed, had become a frequent visitor to Middlecote Hall, Needlewick. She enjoyed the drive, the change of scenery and the insularity of life at the Hall; and, from her vantage point there, could venture forth to sample at first hand all the goings-on of a village whose inhabitants were as familiar to her as when she had lived there as a child. Besides, Deborah felt that it was her duty to go often. She was needed at the Hall. Her sister, Lady Jane Middlecote, could be dreary without Deborah's energetic pursuit of diversion.

During this year's Whitsun visit, it became apparent that there was much of interest afoot.

The sisters ordered tea in the drawing-room, safe in the knowledge that Sir George had absented himself for the day, and they might therefore enjoy several hours of uninterrupted conversation. Deborah established herself in the bay window, thereby gaining a lookout over the valley and, to the east, the village.

"And how is poor George?" she demanded.

"Still too heavy, I'm afraid. I do worry. He gets

terribly puffy-looking, even after just a little exercise or a glass of port."

"But he won't be moderate, I suppose? Gerald was the same."

There was a sombre pause for Gerald's memory to be decently celebrated between the sisters, during which Deborah's eye fell on the chair-backs.

"You decided on the new antimacassars, then? I think white is the right choice — cream would soon have looked tired."

"Yes, I'm very pleased with them. I leave George's old one tucked down the side of his chair for the evenings. I don't want to have them washed too often."

Deborah's attention had strayed to the garden which looked just as it should for May; its borders, arbours and paths pleasing to the eye but unremarkable. Every aspect of Jane's life had that same air of neatness, care and quality — only imagination lacked.

"The river looks very full."

"Yes, we've had so much rain. It flooded earlier in the month nearly to the bridge."

Distant Roundstones, squat behind its white wall, had been encompassed by Deborah's gaze. "And how is Margaret?"

Lady Middlecote crossed to her work-table and removed her knitting; fine wool on slender needles. "Look what I'm making for the bazaar, Deborah. It's a shawl."

"You'll ruin your eyes doing such close work. They'll only sell it for a shilling or two, you'll see. You might just as well have knitted something thick and service-able." The lace shawl hung like a cobweb against Jane's fingers.

"I enjoy it. Some girl will appreciate it, I'm sure." Jane settled herself near the window. "Now, what were we saying?"

"Margaret, Harry — are they well?"

"Oh Harry is much as ever. Yes, they're both well. But Margaret is in a flutter. Sophia Theobald is coming to stay on Saturday for several days."

"*Sophia!* Really?"

Lady Middlecote ran her finger along the close print of the pattern, twined the yarn once round her third finger, twice round the middle, over the index, knitted a stitch, wound the wool three times round the needle.

"She's coming to collect the diary, then? John wrote to her, I suppose," Deborah suggested at last, exasperated by the delay. Jane was deliberately making her wait for information.

"Of course. He had to, as he was the executor. But Margaret says Sophia is coming mainly because she is so soon to be married and wishes to see her relations first."

"Nonsense, the girl has no family feeling whatever."

"How long is it since she was here?"

"I can tell you exactly. She came to Catherine's wedding in August 1909. What a day! Do you remember the thunderstorm? Of course all the Callwoods were invited and as Sophia was staying they brought her. Poor Helen, I did feel sorry for her."

"Why?"

"I'm sure Sophia was too much for her. I don't think Helen ever recovered from that visit, she was never satisfied after that."

"But she's had a very pleasant life. She's certainly got what she wanted."

"You think so? You think so? I wonder."

Deborah's eye was still on Roundstones.

"So Sophia is coming to Needlewick! She won't find it much changed, will she? A few male faces gone. No Helen to bully."

"She didn't bully Helen."

"Of course she did. Helen was asking to be bullied. Don't you remember? I remember her to this day at the wedding breakfast; she never took her eyes from Sophia's face, she was always seeking her approval. She worshipped her! It must have driven Sophia mad. In the end, though, I suppose it did Helen good, made her grow up a bit."

There was a sudden, tense little pause broken hurriedly by Jane.

"I'm afraid Margaret will wear herself out getting the house ready. She's starting on the spare room this morning."

"How inconsiderate of Sophia to have given so little notice! She should have realised Margaret would get in a state."

"How could she know? They can't have met since the brother's funeral and I remember Margaret saying then that Sophia was so distraught she could hardly talk to anyone. She was very fond of her brother."

"We'll call on Margaret this afternoon," Deborah Parditer announced decisively, "and try to calm her down. She'll drive Harry mad by Saturday otherwise."

Roundstones was a white, asymmetrical house set well apart from Needlewick. The lane which ran westwards along the valley climbed steeply away from the village parallel to the River Needle and passed only feet from the front door and wide oriel window of Roundstones. The house, lying high and isolated on the side of the valley, commanded sweeping views across to the Hall and Needlewick, and in the other direction the path of the river could be traced for some considerable distance. The garden fell steeply away, neatly bordered by a high stone wall as if to keep house and grounds from tumbling headlong into the river. At the lower end of the wall, beyond the smooth lawn and wide flowerbeds was a little green door giving access to the river path and the footbridge. The house had been the home of Needlewick doctors for several generations now — and when the previous incumbent had died the house had of course gone to his eldest daughter, Margaret, and her new husband, Dr Harry Callwood.

The housekeeper answered the door to Lady Middlecote and her sister, her fleshy features betraying neither surprise, pleasure, nor indeed displeasure, at their arrival. "She's in the drawing-room," she said at once.

The sisters walked through the small hall to the back room where Margaret Callwood was at the mantelpiece wiping her collection of china cats with a damp cloth. She turned guiltily to face her visitors as if caught in some underhand activity.

"I thought I'd just run a cloth over as Sophia's coming — did Jane tell you? But how are you, Deborah? You do look well! What a delightful hat, I haven't seen it before. How was the drive? Has Mrs Bubb gone for tea, do you think? Perhaps I should help her, we've been so busy. The spare room needed quite a going over, it's been unused for so long."

Deborah Parditer gave her hat a gratified pat and seated herself in an armchair near the window. "I would sit down if I were you, Margaret. You look as if you could do with a rest. I'm quite sure Mrs Bubb is capable of bringing it in herself. You don't want to upset her."

But Margaret still wavered at the door wondering how best to avoid offending Mrs Bubb.

"The garden is looking wonderful, Margaret," added kind Jane Middlecote. "I was telling Deborah that it's particularly splendid this year."

The lure was irresistible; Margaret moved at once to the window. "Yes, I think it does. It was the April rain.

I'm particularly pleased with the azaleas, they're so brilliant."

"The garden is a delight! Sophia has chosen just the right time to come. Now I hope you're not going to overdo it, Margaret, you look a little pale. She's only your niece."

"I do feel rather alarmed. Oh, Mrs Bubb, how kind! Do let me!" Margaret darted from her chair to hold the door back. Tea was laid efficiently, though gracelessly, by Mrs Bubb who picked up the discarded china cloth before closing the door behind her. "Oh dear. She cleaned in here this morning, but she's never liked the cats. And Sophia, I mean she was rather grand when she was only thirteen, and now, marrying into the peerage — and anyway, I'd put myself out for poor Suzanna's daughter, you know I would."

"I suppose you've heard nothing from your sister?" Deborah asked, as she removed the teapot lid from her hostess's preoccupied grasp, stirred the leaves and poured the tea.

"Not a word, no, not since Christmas. Oh thank you, Deborah. Yes, three lumps. And do have a scone — I don't know how Mrs Bubb found the time. You see she doesn't like Sophia, and that makes it worse."

"But the girl hasn't been here for years. How can Mrs Bubb not like her?"

"I know, I know. I think she found her very trying that time, you know. There was always a bit of an atmosphere because Sophia wasn't used to helping out with meals or with her bed, and Mrs Bubb isn't one to forget. And she misses Helen so much, I think she somehow grudges Sophia's visit because she's not Helen."

"I understand John wrote to Sophia about the Will?"

"Oh yes, but I'm sure she's not coming for that. Good Lord, I hope she doesn't bother with that old diary of Helen's, I can't imagine it could have any interest for her.

I really cannot understand Eleanor, it's such an extra-ordinary thing to have done."

"For John's sake," murmured Jane, "I'm glad Sophia is coming to collect the wretched diary. It'll be all finished with then."

"I wish she wouldn't. I wish she wouldn't!" Margaret suddenly exclaimed. "I wish she wouldn't read it."

3

SOPHIA TRAVELLED TO Needlewick by train, but this time alone. She sat by the window in a first class compartment, a small gladstone bag in the rack above her head, and smiled at her elusive reflection in the window as she recalled her previous trip to Needlewick. Perched opposite then had been Miss Pinner, governess, whom Sophia had always insisted should be designated "companion". Sophia could still recall the irritation of being in Miss Pinner's proximity, the violent distaste she had felt for the woman's sad brown hair, large yellow front teeth and wide mouth that never closed. My God, I must have been a terrible charge, she reflected, my nerves screaming when she touched me, every ounce of ingenuity directed at making her life as unpleasant as possible. I don't suppose I spoke once all the way on the train, or even said goodbye at Cheltenham. I believe I may even have tipped her! The memory of this insult caused Sophia to shift in the seat and turn away from the window. And the luggage I insisted on bringing with me — all those dresses, and no one at home with the energy to dissuade me. They just let me bring it all. Still, Helen appreciated it. Sophia could remember Helen's long hair dangling over the side of the trunk as she peered at the London finery.

Sophia was tired. Arranging this visit had been exhausting because she had felt considerable reluctance, a desire to hold back. And her father was irritable all week at the prospect of her return to Needlewick. She admitted to Colin that she could understand why even the name of the place must be painful to her father, but added: "For heaven's sake, it was my mother's home, and I haven't got so many relations that I can afford to ignore them altogether."

Because she was excluding Colin she had treated him with unusual kindness during the week prior to her departure, grateful for his ready belief in her excuses. "My aunt is a great worrier, you see. It would kill her to have to entertain a real peer. She'd think she ought to slaughter a swan from the Needle at the very least!"

"She'll have to meet me some day."

"Yes, at the wedding, but that won't be nearly such an ordeal for her, there'll be so many people."

So now she was travelling to Needlewick alone, the weight of being someone's daughter, someone's betrothed temporarily left behind. The train steamed through frothy May embankments, woods floating on the purple haze of bluebells, bright, eager green fields. Wonderful train taking me away, taking me away, taking me away. . . .

She was touched that both her uncle and aunt should have taken the trouble to come to the station to meet her; it seemed surprising that they should endow her visit with any significance. There was the inevitable awkwardness of a first meeting after two years but her aunt was never short of words for long. "Harry's got a motor car," she announced. "It's so useful for a country doctor, though he's always getting it stuck on farm tracks. He won't learn." Sophia was moved by the warmth of her embrace and the brightness of her smile. She reflected suddenly that Needlewick must be a dull and lonely place for her aunt now Helen had left and Eleanor Gresham was dead.

They sat crushed together in the back of the car; the flow of Margaret's conversation unimpeded by the noise of the engine. Sophia leaned against the hard seat and watched the high-banked lanes jolt past, remembering her former visit. The trip from the station in an open trap under heavy drizzle; the sharp pain at the base of her neck as her collar became soaked; and the sense of dragging despair as the chestnut horses pulled her further and further from the station, from Nicholas and from her mother.

"I thought I'd come," her aunt confided. "I had some shopping in Cheltenham. It's so unlike Harry to offer to bring me. You know, Sophia, we were thrilled to hear of your engagement. Lady Kilbride sounds very grand, doesn't it? How will you like being called that? I wish Helen would marry. She's getting old now. Well, of course I know you're older and the war came — so many young men. . . . But it seems odd for her to be with all those women."

"How is Helen?" Sophia shouted. "I'm longing to hear all about her. She sounds quite brilliant."

"Oh she is, she is! But it's a strange life for a girl. I keep hoping she'll decide to be a teacher after all and come back to a local school. But she doesn't seem to want to leave Cambridge. I say Harry, do watch these bends! He goes so fast!"

Her ready, feminine conversation was restful to Sophia who watched her with affection. She studied her aunt's face for some resemblance to her mother, but found none except in the bone structure of nose and chin. Aunt Margaret was quite plump and still incurably untidy; modern clothes did not become her at all, and brown had never suited her. Sophia noted that her hair was still worn in an untidy chignon with the inevitable wispy grey strands escaping from under her hat.

Harry had a call to make in Needlewick, and wondered if the ladies would mind walking to Roundstones from the village — he'd bring the luggage later. This was not what Sophia had planned, she had wanted her first walk to be alone, not with chattering Aunt Margaret, but she responded: "Of course I shall enjoy the walk. And I'm so looking forward to seeing Roundstones again."

They were dropped at the bottom of the High Street.

"I expect you'll notice plenty of changes, Sophia. Even Needlewick cannot quite escape the modern world."

Sophia was disappointed, for, despite her unpropitiously damp arrival that first summer, her imagination had retained a picture of Needlewick floating like a watercolour in an eternal mist of hot blue days. But on this cloudy May afternoon of her return it seemed rather an unremarkable little village distinguished only by its fine Norman church on the hill. The surface of the High Street had been repaired; the chickens had gone from the yard of the Makepeace cottage and near the church now stood a new white cenotaph.

"It seems much smaller, things always do," she remarked, shivering. "And it was always so hot when I was here last. I suppose it can't have been every day."

"We've had some lovely days this spring. We can't really complain."

"That's where the Makepeace family lived, isn't it? I remember the name. Are they still there?"

"Some. Two of the boys were killed in the war — another came back not quite right. One of the girls is married, another in service. There are only two at home now."

"Were there only six then? There seemed to be hundreds of children."

"There were others. Some died. We had a spate of infant deaths in the village before the war — your uncle suspected the water."

But Makepeace children ought not to die, ought not to grow up and fight in wars. They stand forever in cottage doorways, extending filthy hands for raspberry drops and grinning toothily at well-dressed visitors from London.

The two women crossed the bridge and began to climb towards Roundstones.

"Does Mrs Bubb still work for you?"

"Oh good heavens yes, she's a dear. I couldn't manage without her."

"I'm afraid she and I didn't quite see eye to eye when I was last here."

"Oh, I don't know. You were only a child."

They had just rounded a slight bend. Sophia stopped. A man sat on a gate beside the lane, stripping the seeds from a sheaf of grasses. He smiled at her.

"Michael!"

He doffed his cap, but did not get off the gate.

Her aunt took her elbow and ushered her along.

"I expect Mrs Bubb will have a lovely steak and kidney pudding for supper, we usually have steak and kidney on a Thursday!" Margaret spoke in a high, loud voice until they were well out of earshot. "You remember him then?" she whispered at last.

"Yes. He used to work for Uncle Harry, didn't he? I'd recognise him anywhere. Does he still work at Roundstones?"

"No — oh no!"

"I was surprised to see him. I would have thought he'd

be the sort to get away as soon as possible."

"No — he's never left Needlewick."

"Not even in the war?"

"No, he wasn't called up — medical reasons. He stayed here, working as a labourer. They were all desperate for men. I should keep out of his way, Sophia."

"Don't worry, I shall. He always was a bit odd."

"Yes, he's odd. Just a little. I don't like to spread gossip, but you should be warned."

And now they could see Roundstones tucked into the hillside, its oriel window blindly reflecting the outside afternoon. "I had forgotten what a lovely house it is!" Sophia exclaimed. "And the view!"

They paused to look down the valley towards the Needle.

"Is the bridge still there? And the path by the river?"

"You do have a good memory. Yes, the path's probably overgrown now. I don't use it much. The road's so much more convenient for the village."

But the path Sophia remembered went in another direction.

"I expect you could do with a nice cup of tea. Come in, come in, dear. You're in the room you had before. I always leave Helen's in case she might drop by on impulse. Mrs Bubb — Mrs Bubb! We're back."

Sophia knew from the previous visit that bells were never rung in Roundstones. If Mrs Bubb's services were required, Helen or Aunt Margaret used to creep to the kitchen, knock on the door and murmur: "I'm sorry to disturb you, Mrs Bubb, but would you mind . . ."

And here she was, lumbering up the passage, her skirts fractionally shorter, her hair thinner but otherwise little changed.

"Hello!" Sophia exclaimed. "I've been so looking

forward to seeing you again!" The words splintered at her feet in hollow shards. Mrs Bubb eyed her with scorn and announced: "I've set the tea in the drawing-room." Sophia had no delusions about the housekeeper's opinion of her: over-dressed, over-indulged, indolent and affected.

But despite Mrs Bubb's hostility Sophia was happy. The smell of Roundstones: fresh green scent from the gardens, beeswax, old books, stone flags; the dark room; the hot tea and wonderful, thickly buttered scones; her aunt's interminable flow of observations and questions. All was as it should be.

I was happy here, Sophia thought, until the end, and I didn't realise. I have not been happy since. I cried and suffered here, but at least I was alive, at least I felt. I haven't really felt much since, not even about my mother, not even about Nicholas's death. Those more recent events seemed to happen at a distance. Here everything was immediate, or perhaps it was because I was a child then, and have since grown up.

"But you must tell me about your plans, all your wonderful news," insisted her aunt. "I was so flattered, Sophia, that you should think to come to Needlewick before your marriage."

Sophia was too ashamed of her long years of neglect to discuss Mr Gresham's letter. "Yes, I felt I must come back. I'm sorry I never made time before."

"Oh, we wouldn't expect it! You've been far too busy — your poor father must have needed you, a great comfort to him . . ." Margaret skimmed away from discussing the one who always hovered, ghost-like, behind a mention of Simon Theobald. "So tell me about your fiancé. What's it like to be engaged to a lord?"

In this drawing-room, with its old chintz and polished boards, Sophia had yawned through so many tea-times, studied each volume on the shelves in the hope of finding amusement, sat apparently absorbed by letters from home in the hope that her preoccupation would ward off Mrs Bubb or Aunt Margaret. Boredom is such a luxury, she reflected now. It's such a simple discomfort. I wish now I was only bored, then I wouldn't have to lie.

"I suppose I don't think much about the title."

"Of course, of course, I'm so silly! Forgive me."

"No, no! It does sound rather grand, doesn't it? He's very good to me, much more than I deserve. I'm afraid he spoils me."

"That's as it should be. I remember when your uncle and I became engaged he'd always bring me something; a few flowers, a card, a book."

It seemed strange to imagine gentle Aunt Margaret in the throes of a love affair. Colin had never brought Sophia a little posy or chosen a book for her. His presents were lavish: a great sheaf of carnations, Swiss chocolates, silk. "I sometimes wish he wouldn't," she admitted, and then made an extraordinary admission — to her aunt, of all people. "Aunt Margaret, sometimes I wonder if I'm right to marry him."

She laughed: "All girls have qualms before they marry. After all, it's a big step. A very big step — you must be sure. Now have you chosen a dress?"

There was no help then. Sophia let the moment pass. "I'm very fond of ivory. And my mother carried white flowers. So shall I."

"Yes, I remember, I have a photograph. Oh, Suzanna on her wedding day! I had spring flowers. We married in the spring."

Sophia, ill at ease in this discussion of weddings, laid her palms on her knees and said brightly: "And now that's enough of my news. Please tell me about Helen and what's been happening in Needlewick."

"Eleanor's dead," Margaret replied at once. "Eleanor

has died. Oh, of course you know. I miss her so, she was my dearest friend."

"I felt very sorry for Mr Gresham when I met him."

"Yes, poor man. He's managed so well. But they knew for years that she was very sick — they found out soon after they were married, he told us. And they never said a word, not even to Harry."

Sophia could not bear to listen. "And now Helen? You must be so proud of her."

"Oh we are, we are! She has done wonderfully well for a girl."

"Do you visit her often?"

"Occasionally, yes. But she's so busy. I never could have imagined Helen in one of those places. Of course I can't begin to take in what it is she studies. Mathematics always seemed such an odd choice for her. She loved pictures and stories when she was a very little girl."

"I would like to see her again. We hardly spoke at Nicholas's service."

"You had other things to think about then, dear, we understood."

"I wrote to her and told her I was going to be married. She didn't reply."

"I expect she didn't have time. She's always so busy. So many books, students. . . ."

The doctor's voice could be heard in the kitchen.

"I'll go and help with my bag," Sophia offered, "and have a wash."

"Yes, how selfish of me to keep you talking after your journey." Aunt Margaret began to collect the tea things.

Sophia met her uncle in the hall and took her luggage from him. He looked very weary.

"That's right, don't let him carry them heavy bags. You go and sit down, Doctor, I'll bring a cup of tea." Mrs Bubb chivvied him into the drawing-room and Sophia began slowly to mount the stairs. On her way along the landing she passed the closed door of Helen's room and then came to the spare room which was even more cluttered than she remembered. It had obviously become the repository for old books, knick-knacks and small items of furniture. The coverlet was glaringly modern, a loud floral pattern, probably purchased at a garden party. There were flowers on the bedside table.

She went at once to the window which looked out over the garden. There was the little gate and beyond the wall the willow tree by the river. The greyness of the afternoon and the attractive but unremarkable view almost made her weep, for it held none of the enchantment endowed by memory. No Helen in a grimy flounced pinafore stood on the terrace calling her name, there was no invitation to shared secrets under the willow.

A small mirror stood on the chest-of-drawers and in it Sophia caught a glimpse of her elegant, adult form. We had such lovely clothes in those days, she thought, or at least I did, not poor Helen, dressed in cast-offs and peculiar home-made frocks. Mine were all tucked and embroidered and starched. She smiled, remembering Mrs Bubb's opinion of those creations. Now Mrs Bubb — she had not changed. She at least was constant. Listening, Sophia could hear the housekeeper's heavy tread in the passage between kitchen and dining-room, otherwise house and garden were quiet. A blackbird on the lawn cocked its head. The wind lifted the skirts of the willow.

4

SOPHIA HAD NOT planned for rain in Needlewick for, apart from the day of her arrival, it had been dry and fine throughout her previous visit. Except of course on the day of the wedding. Ah yes, they had gone to a wedding, and the thunder had ricochetted through the church with such force that the candles flickered. Helen had clutched Sophia's hand, afraid. But the wedding had not been in Needlewick; there the lanes were crisply rutted with dry mud the colour of Helen's hair, and cows had stood in yellowed grass angrily flicking their tails.

Sophia had forgotten how small and dark Roundstones was, how little there would be to do. How had she stuck it before? With bad grace, she imagined, although at least then Helen had provided company. Now there was only Aunt Margaret, determined to entertain her guest properly whilst obviously in a fidget to return to her usual Friday routine.

"Aunt, please let me help you clear the table," Sophia said after breakfast.

"No, I won't hear of it, you are on holiday. I'll just take these to the kitchen for Mrs Bubb and then we'll go to the drawing-room. I have a few photographs of Helen you might like to see — there's one of her graduation."

"Come on now, let me load the tray. I remember Mrs Bubb was quite annoyed when I was here before, all pampered and refusing to lift a finger."

They both laughed a little consciously.

"She does look remarkably well," Sophia commented. "I always thought of her as really old, the way one does as a child, but she seems just the same. And I mean she was housekeeper here when you and mama were children, wasn't she?"

"She's part of Roundstones and she doesn't change though perhaps she's slowed up. I'll just take these through now. Please, Sophia, you go and sit down."

Sophia wandered across the hall to the drawing-room where the windows overlooked the dripping garden. So much for nostalgic rambles, for communing with the lost days of her childhood and finding solace in the quiet valley of the Needle!

But by lunch-time she was ready to disregard the weather. Aunt Margaret was a good companion for an hour, unutterably tedious for longer. Sophia was hungry for her mother's name to be spoken, for her aunt to indulge in reminiscences about her childhood or even to discuss Helen further, but apparently there were to be no confidences, only chat about the forthcoming flower festival and fête, and the state of Harry's practice. Margaret wanted to hear about Sophia's wedding plans but, at Roundstones, cloaked by rain, the wedding was a mere pinprick at the wrong end of a telescope; the marriage of another Sophia, a smart, beautiful London Sophia who didn't yawn achingly behind her hand at ten a.m. or remember with a peculiar twist of the heart the row of books in the glass case which had not changed in eleven years. I know, she realised suddenly, that, if I put my hand in and reach for the one with green binding third from the left, it will be *The Wide, Wide World*.

"I think I must go for a walk this afternoon — regardless of the rain," Sophia remarked at lunch.

"But it's pouring. I'm sure it will be better tomorrow. And Jane Middlecote said she might call this afternoon."

"Oh I'll be back by four. I don't mind the rain, really. Lovely clean country rain, so unlike the murk of London."

"Well you must take my galoshes and you can have Harry's old umbrella. Where will you go?"

"I thought down to the river and into Needlewick across the fields. I'll call on Mr Gresham."

"Oh yes, for the diary. Fancy Eleanor leaving you that! So strange. I can't understand why she thought you would want Helen's childish scribblings."

"Would you like to see it?" Sophia enquired gently.

"Oh no, no. No! I won't delve into the past, such a foolish thing to do. Live in the present, that's what I say."

"I'm sure it's safer," Sophia agreed.

She took the umbrella and even obediently donned the galoshes before leaving Roundstones by the garden door. The rain was soft, a caress, and the air lush with the scent of grass and sodden roses. The willow was a fountain of wet leaves; she parted the branches and peered into the green cave within.

The path beside the river meandered upstream muddily and uninvitingly. That way lay the Tunnel Woods. Sophia turned hurriedly and made for the little footbridge and the path up the valley towards Middlecote Hall.

The rain had grown heavier by the time she reached the village so she paid a reluctant visit to the church, although the dim interior of St John's would offer little warmth. But at the porch she found her way barred by a pair of outstretched legs. They did not move to let her pass, but their owner, who was lolling on a narrow stone bench, said: "I thought you'd remember me. I never forgot you."

"No."

"I knew you'd come back one day."

"Goodness! How are you, Michael?"

"Oh not so bad, not so bad."

"I was just on my way to visit Mr Gresham."

"He's not in. He rarely is on a weekday afternoon any more."

"Ah — well, never mind."

Now that she had an opportunity to study him more closely she saw that Michael was still very small, thin-faced and bony, even less prepossessing as an adult than as a child. Already his hair was thinning and his pronounced teeth discoloured.

"Staying long, are you?"

"Not very, no."

She wanted to escape, but could not step over his legs and was too proud to retreat back along the path without an excuse.

"Well, I'll try Mr Gresham and then I really must be getting back."

He stood up, fell in beside her and asked conversationally: "So what have you been doing all these years?"

"Oh, growing up. I'm engaged," she told him desperately. "And you?"

"The same."

He held the lych-gate open, forcing her to walk very close to him as she passed through.

"Well, I mustn't keep you," she said.

"Oh, I've nothing much on. I don't often get the chance to speak to the bride-to-be of a lord."

How did he know? They came to The Grey House, where Mr Gresham's servant, a newcomer, said he was out but was expecting her to call, perhaps on Saturday.

When she turned back to the road, Michael had gone.

As she walked rapidly down the High Street she speculated on what he wanted with her — he could not be trusted to have a simple motive for he had been a frightening child given to lurking close at hand and appearing at unlikely moments. Indeed, such was the force of one particular memory of Michael that Sophia stumbled suddenly, as if caught in a mighty gust of wind. She could see again, clearly, Michael's boyish hand and grubby face, there in the clearing, in the leaves, and Helen's body rigid, her face transfixed.

They were awaiting her in the drawing-room: her aunt, Lady Middlecote whose strangely neutral quality she remembered well, and a heavy-chested woman with eager, inquiring eyes. Jarred by her recent encounter, Sophia was momentarily caught off balance by the current of expectation in the room and her usually assured smile was shaky.

"Ah, here she is at last!" cried Aunt Margaret, ushering her into the room and touching her hair. "I hope you didn't get too wet. I was telling them you would not be kept indoors."

"Lady Middlecote. How lovely to see you again." Sophia's well modulated voice was controlled.

Lady Middlecote shook her hand, kissed her cheek and introduced her to her sister, Mrs Deborah Parditer, who said: "You won't recognise me, of course, but you came to my daughter's wedding. I remember you well. I see you've fined down — don't get as thin as your mother! And you've resisted the temptation to cut your hair!"

"Oh yes," Sophia responded politely, ignoring the intimacy of Mrs Parditer's last comments, "I remember, there was a thunderstorm. And is your daughter well?"

"Very. She has three children of her own now."

"And you, Sophia? You are to be married. We were all so pleased to hear the news," smiled Lady Middlecote, embracing Sophia once more in her soft arms and bosom. "I always knew you were destined for great things. I remember you handing out the prizes at our garden party, so composed and magnanimous for so small a girl."

"It is Helen who has been successful!" Sophia exclaimed. "I have merely found a wealthy husband. She must have worked terribly hard — for a woman she's done extremely well, don't you think?"

"Your father must be very pleased," observed Mrs Parditer obviously determined that the subject of Sophia's marriage should not yet be dismissed.

"Yes, he is. Very. I'm a fortunate young lady," replied Sophia coolly.

"And what does your mama think?"

"You must be more than ready for tea, Sophia," interposed Margaret. "Are you sure you're not damp — perhaps you should change your shoes?"

"They're quite dry. I wore your galoshes and, unlike last time I was here, I came properly equipped with strong shoes. My mother has not written for some time," Sophia added, returning Mrs Parditer's direct gaze. "I was wondering in fact whether she might have written to one of you? Or perhaps Mrs Gresham? I know they were very close at one time."

Lady Middlecote, whose eyes had met Margaret's, seized the opportunity to change the subject. "Of course you've heard of our loss. Our dear friend. But I believe she left you something."

Sophia realised wearily that everyone in Needlewick must know about the diary. "Yes, I'm amazed she remembered me."

"Oh Eleanor would never forget anyone. Never. She

was very wise, such a loss to us all."

There was a pause and then Aunt Margaret said: "You see, Sophia, she was an invalid for so long and towards the end reading or sewing or even talking tired her. It's no wonder some of her ideas were a little strange — she had so many hours of enforced inactivity."

"Do you suppose she was ill then, even when I was in Needlewick all those years ago?"

"Oh yes. Oh yes, she knew long before then."

Sophia remembered Mrs Gresham on her bicycle, free wheeling, her light dress flying, her hair loosened beneath her hat. "She used to ride a bicycle," she murmured.

"Yes, she loved that machine. She gave it to Helen before the war. She couldn't ride it then."

"Poor John," sighed Lady Middlecote. "Poor man! He was devoted to her."

"And yet it must be a relief. He must feel worn out after all those years with an invalid."

Margaret, who seemed to find this conversation particularly painful began to fuss about the tea: "Mrs Bubb is very late! I'll go and help her, I know she's been busy with some late spring cleaning in the scullery."

"No, let me, I insist. You sit still, Aunt!" Sophia could not stand the scrutiny of Mrs Parditer and her sister any longer. She was an invader in such a tight little group that she could feel herself being consumed by their craving for novelty. She placed her hands on her aunt's shoulders, pressed her firmly back into the chair, and escaped.

"Oh she's so beautiful," murmured Jane Middlecote the instant the door was closed, "I never thought she would be such a beauty."

"She's nothing like her mother, though," replied her

sister, "she has none of Suzanna's delicacy."

"But she's so much easier now. She's lost all her little airs and graces. She doesn't seem to mind how homely we are here," Margaret said.

"She's very reluctant to talk about her wedding," remarked Deborah sharply. "She's hardly my idea of the blushing bride."

"Girls are so much more sophisticated now, not like us."

"Does she speak much about her mother, Margaret?"

"I don't like to bring up the subject. I know her father wouldn't like it, and I feel I'd inevitably be taking sides."

"You mean *you* can't bear to mention Suzanna's name! You'd be doing the girl a great favour, she must be missing her a good deal at present. A girl needs her mother when she is to be married. Not that Suzanna would be any help, I admit."

"Hush, Deborah, please!"

"Oh for goodness sake!" Deborah straightened in her chair and turned her head aside. "I'm surprised the peonies aren't out, Margaret. They're late, aren't they?" Thoughts of Suzanna, and Suzanna's daughter with her steady dark eyes and set, down-turned mouth were so unsettling.

"Yes, they're late, everything is."

This safe topic was seized on with enthusiasm and when Sophia returned, prettily flushed by the unaccustomed task of carrying a laden tray, the three were harmoniously discussing the proper method of dealing with slugs.

5

THE AIR ON a mild May morning in Needlewick was
soupy with the perfume of thrusting blossom and
fresh green foliage. Beyond the garden of Middlecote
Hall the water-meadow was hedged with hawthorn,
elder and knee-high nettles. Cows browsed near the
river, flicking their tails against ubiquitous flies, still, at
six-thirty, a little stupid from the cool of the night.

It was years since Deborah had been down to the river
so early, not indeed since her wedding morning, but she
had woken at four and for once been unable to harness
sleep or drifting thoughts. A blackbird sang persistently
outside her window and in the eaves the youthful contents of a starling's nest hawked so relentlessly for food
that she at last got up, dressed, and let herself out of the
Hall.

But here by the river she found no peace. Here,
Suzanna Gilling, with long blonde hair neatly plaited
under a straw boater, seemed to hang over the little
wooden bridge with her sister and drop sticks into the
water, hers, as always first and fastest.

"Go on, Margaret! Throw yours. You're too slow! Let
it go with the current!"

Then across the water was the willow where the five of them, "The Needlewick Five" as they secretly designated themselves, held their meetings, planned their tea parties and wrote their magazine.

Deborah, then Deborah Henshaw, always kept the minutes which began with a list of "Those Present" and continued with "Apologies for Absence". For years there were seldom Apologies, and then more and more often: Suzanna Gilling, Suzanna, Suzanna . . .

Next came the Officers' Reports — each girl held an Office, even little Jane. First Suzanna, the Chairman, spoke — since she had invented the club she must be its driving force and organiser. Her report dwelt on past achievements and future pleasures: "We are pleased to report that Eleanor Carney has embarked on the study of Latin with her father the Reverend James Carney and can already decline the verb to love. . . . (Go on Eleanor, go on. . . .) Jane and Deborah have completed their samplers; we regret that Jane's is rather grubby, but know she will do better next time. Despite Deborah's incessant moans she has as usual achieved perfection. Margaret — what have you been up to, Meg? — Oh yes, her radishes didn't go woody this year . . . And I — I have completed the entire Brontë works and am about to start on Mrs Gaskell.

"As a society The Needlewick Five left surprise food parcels for three villagers and [lowered voice] actually achieved its long-held ambition to meet at midnight under the willow [giggles]. For future plans see 'Any Other Business'. Yes, yes, I've got a wonderful idea, but first, the Treasurer's report. Margaret?"

Out came Margaret's pocket book, carefully ruled, every farthing meticulously entered or subtracted. It was a rule that each girl should contribute half her pocket money.

Eleanor was "Village Affairs Correspondent".

"The main event was the wedding of George Make-peace, aged twenty, to Helen Greene, aged sixteen, on Saturday 26 April. The bride wore a pale grey gown in sprigged cotton and carried primroses. The Needlewick Five gathered at the lych-gate to throw rice. . . ."

Secretary — Deborah? "No letters received, but one sent to Mrs Bubb at Roundstones thanking her for her kind contribution to the April picnic. . . ."

"Honorary President, that's you, Jane — nothing to report? Good, then on to 'Any Other Business'. Now then, the May picnic — The Tunnel Woods!"

"But Suzanna, we went there last year!"

"I know. But this year" . . . dramatic pause . . . "we're going *into* the Tunnel."

Mrs Deborah Parditer stood on the footbridge and gazed upstream towards those same woods.

Suzanna would not be kept away from them. Needle-wick, set in a valley, was close to so much woodland that trees, bluebells, ferns, woodland paths held no special allure for The Needlewick Five. Generally they preferred open spaces, though they were familiar with most of the local tracks and bridle ways. The Henshaw girls rode daily and were so familiar with the area that they could have gone blindfold down overgrown paths and known precisely where to duck their heads. But they never rode to the Tunnel Woods which were, besides being private property, too dark and steep to attract girls on horseback.

But The Needlewick Five went there one year, as a result of Suzanna's lust for novelty, when Deborah, the eldest, was thirteen and Jane, the youngest, seven. Suzanna, as usual, had got her way, by fielding their objections with a quick smile and deft retorts none of them could resist. First cool-headed Eleanor would be coaxed on to her side, then sister Margaret and finally the reluctant, and, in Deborah's case, sulky, Henshaw girls. And to the Tunnel Woods they went.

They had, in previous years, picnicked by the river and clambered up a steep path through the trees until they came to the mouth of a Tunnel, a folly, Mrs Bubb up at Roundstones had later informed them, cut through the rock by a previous owner with a taste for the Gothic. But, although they had returned several times, the girls had never ventured inside the Tunnel. It was too dark, too narrow, and always a little too late to explore further.

But now, when Suzanna had said, "And this time we will go *into* the Tunnel," a little thrill had passed through the group because go they would, following Suzanna's trim, determined figure, up the steep path and into the Tunnel and heaven knew what mysteries and excitement, and there could be no turning back.

And who could say, Mrs Deborah Parditer now thought, if things might have turned out better or worse without that trip to the Tunnel Woods with two baskets of food — chicken sandwiches and apples packed at Roundstones — and their strongest shoes?

Suzanna sang: *"Where are you going to my pretty maid?"* and took little bouncing skips on the chorus, *"Sir, she said, Sir, she said. . . .* Come on, girls, join in!" The river was clear and quick and the sun hot on their gloved hands. Suzanna would have drifted away anyway, Deborah acknowledged, we could not hold her. She made too many demands that we could never satisfy.

And now the daughter, Sophia, was at Roundstones, waking in her mother's old room. What did she hope to find in Needlewick?

The clock in the tower of St John's struck the quarter, announcing that breakfast would be served. Jane would

—38—

not be down yet and Deborah did not much relish Sir George's company. He would slurp his tea and attempt conversation when he had much better be silent. But she was too hungry to wait any longer.

6

AT BREAKFAST ON Saturday there was a note for Sophia from Mr Gresham inviting her to call at eleven.

"But I'm sure you need not go today," Aunt Margaret said. "I wondered if you'd like a drive, Harry's free this morning. You could go later — one evening perhaps."

But Sophia would not be put off — the diary was waiting for her — she could almost feel it calling, and she could not resist.

The morning was dazzling and already the hedgerows were warm, exuding a tickly, burnt-grass scent from the cow parsley. There seemed to be so much space and light that Sophia wondered why she had neglected to come back before. But really she meant that she was at last alone. No man pursued her activities, not her father, not Colin. She gave a tiny dance, a girl again, swinging her arms, lifting her pale face to the sunshine.

The High Street was quite lively for Needlewick and she smiled benignly at curious faces turned towards her. She recognised none of them, though probably by now most knew who she was. When she came to the little lane which led to the Greshams' old grey house near the church the memory of that hot garden wall, smelling softly of stone and earth, was so powerful that she thought: If I go quietly and enter by the garden door she will be there, seated under the apple tree. But the garden was empty and overgrown and in the french windows stood Mr Gresham, apparently waiting for her.

"It's in my study," he said at once. "We'll fetch it."

The house was very still and already a kind of masculine gloom had settled. Eleanor had gone and with her delicacy and brightness. They did not speak as they crossed the hall as if in fear of waking a sleeping child.

His study was a dark, north-facing room; with a sudden flush of affection she realised that he had probably chosen it so that his wife could sit in the light rooms facing the garden. The shelves were laden with legal volumes, quarterly magazines and haphazard piles of papers. On the desk, she saw at once, was a photograph of a stiff couple, she in a white, voluminous dress, he standing to attention behind her.

"She never let me take any photographs," he remarked softly. "This is all I have."

"Why, why ever not?"

"She said she wouldn't have me record her slow decline. She thought my memories would be enough. Perhaps she's right. And here is the diary. It seems hardly worth your coming all this way for this."

There were two cheap red exercise books, well thumbed. On the covers, in faded ink, was carefully inscribed the name: Helen Margaret Callwood.

"There were others, earlier ones, I believe, but my wife kept only these."

Tucked into one was a little folded slip of paper. The words inside were scrawled as if with a damaged pen: *"For Sophia. Don't forget. From Eleanor Gresham, February 1920."*

"Oh this is your note, surely," she said.

"No, she told me to give it to you. She was very particular about all the things she left. She was very careful. She had lots of time to plan, you see."

They both stood awkwardly by the desk, and then he said hurriedly: "I expect you're in a rush to get back, but it's so hot, perhaps you'd like a glass of lemonade, or sherry. Would you?"

She could not leave him to his lonely Saturday morning. "Oh, that would be lovely. Perhaps in the garden? I've never forgotten your garden."

He disappeared down a passage to the kitchen leaving Sophia to wonder why Needlewick residents were always so afraid of their servants.

The garden had of course shrunk. She had remembered it as being boundless but now it seemed to have closed in on itself, huddled up. She found Mrs Gresham's little paved walk to the rose garden where many of the blooms were overblown, the leaves blighted. The apple tree was covered with little hard green fruits.

Presently Mr Gresham appeared with two glasses.

"I'm afraid I know nothing about gardening," he said apologetically. "We have a man who comes a couple of times a week but it doesn't seem to be enough." He set the glasses down carefully on the edge of the garden seat. "I hope this bench won't mark your frock."

"Oh, it's only an old thing!" she replied, safe in the knowledge that he would be ignorant of London fashion.

They sat awkwardly with the diary between them.

"Have you read it?" she asked.

He gave her a quick sideways glance. "Not recently. I believe I did have a look when Helen first gave it to my wife — long before the war."

"I wonder how Helen came to give away something so personal."

He gripped his hands together in his lap. "She stopped visiting us so often, you know. Eleanor was very sorry. And then she went away to school."

"I remember Helen always used to love coming here."

"She grew very tired of Needlewick. I suppose any intelligent young person would."

"Do you recall what you read in the diary?"

Again there was a little pause. "Oh my head has been filled with so many facts since then."

After a moment she asked: "Shall you go on living here, Mr Gresham?" She was watching his hands, still folded firmly, as if he were afraid they would make some desperate gesture if he freed them.

"I don't know, it's such a short while since she died. At the moment I couldn't bear to leave — not when I remember her so vividly. And the summer is worse — I had not expected. . . . She loved the sunshine and the garden."

Sophia said nothing for a while and then ventured: "I'm sure she was very happy."

"She always said so. She always said I made her happy."

At last Sophia touched his hand and stood.

"I'm afraid I must go now. I'm expected back for lunch."

"Yes, yes, of course. I apologise. Of course. I didn't mean to keep you. Thank you."

"It is I who should thank you for keeping these safe for me when you must have had so much else on your mind. Goodbye, Mr Gresham."

"Goodbye, Sophia."

As she closed the garden door softly behind her and walked away she could still feel his cool, dry hand beneath her fingers.

*

In the afternoon she developed a bad headache — so desperate was she to avoid her aunt's plans for tea at Middlecote Hall that the pain became real.

"I must, must lie down, Aunt Margaret. I'm so sorry, it was the sunshine this morning, I expect. My hat hasn't much of a brim."

But Margaret was no fool. She had noticed her niece's bulging pocket when she returned at lunch-time, how she had carried her jacket hurriedly upstairs, and the slight air of confusion when she responded to enquiries about Mr Gresham's health.

At three Margaret left Roundstones to walk slowly through the village to the Hall. The doctor was away on a call and Sophia was alone.

Stifled by the silent house — even Mrs Bubb, it seemed, needed to rest for she had heard the house-keeper's heavy footfall on the stairs to the second floor — she took the diaries down to the willow by the river where the afternoon sun was diffused by the curtain of leaves. She sat comfortably against a nearby trunk, bathed in mellow light, and began to read.

7

Wednesday, 14 July 1909

There was another letter from Aunt Suzanna this morning. Nicholas is far worse. Father tried to reassure me — he said that measles is really very common and most people survive any complications, but mother repeated her fear that my cousin may go blind. I believe she secretly thinks he'll die. Of course we do not know Nicholas at all, but his death would cause such sadness in the family. He's so young.

And Sophia will arrive tomorrow by the three o'clock train. I have been sitting beneath the hawthorn tree all afternoon thinking about her. Up until now I have been unable to grasp that she might actually come. How strange it will be to share my summer. I have no idea what she is like: she is a dream figure to me. All I really know about her is that she is my cousin, has a dying brother and very rich parents.

I have two imaginary pictures of her. One is that she'll be rather like a porcelain statue: delicate and refined, but cold. She will sit all day at the piano in the drawing-room and will hardly speak to me. The other idea I have is that she'll be beautiful, laughing and generous and will love me and be as anxious as I am to be friends. What a perfect summer we would have then.

I'm really terribly nervous about her. All afternoon my thoughts have swung from one possibility to another. Half of me says: she'll ruin my summer, Needlewick is mine, I don't want to share it. She'll cut me off from my people. And then the other half replies: yes, but you may love her, you may find you want to give her everything; and I start planning our days together. I'll show her Needlewick, and the willow, and the church. We'll visit Mrs Gresham, and the Middlecotes, and go to the garden party. I'll have a friend, for the first time, someone to share things with, even, possibly, maybe, my people? Could I?

In the end I made myself quiet. I sat under the hawthorn tree making the most of my last chance of being alone there, as I am now — Helen on her own. I needed to see my people to tell them what is happening, but they didn't come. Of course it was damp, but they must have known I needed them.

I felt sad as I left the clearing and the tree. I had anticipated so many long afternoons there this summer. And now, because of Sophia, I shan't be alone and free to visit when I wish.

I am so muddled and nervous.

In twenty-four hours Sophia will be here. I wonder how I shall be feeling then.

Friday, 16 July
Cousin Sophia has been here a day now. She has changed everything. The house even seems to smell different because she is here.

Yesterday I woke early. Even in my sleep I must have known and remembered she was coming. When I saw the rain I was sad because she would not first see Needlewick in the sunshine. Mother and Mrs Bubb and I were run off our feet all morning. Mother said that Sophia is used to such comfort and elegance that Roundstones will be a shock to her. But how could anyone dislike Roundstones?

I prepared her room. She has new cream muslin curtains and the cushion I've been embroidering in brown and gold cross-stitch is on the bed. I put out the best towels and picked an enormous vase of flowers, all the sweetest smelling. I can't think that she could be used to anything quite so comfortable and elegant as her room then looked.

Mrs Bubb did not seem very excited by Sophia's arrival. In fact, when I was helping her cut scones in the kitchen she was more ill-tempered than usual.

"It'll do that girl the world of good to be out of town, away from all those servants swarming around," she told me. "She'll be spoilt to death, I expect. I daresay she'll hardly know how to dress herself."

"'But she'll be dreadfully homesick," I argued, wondering why Mrs Bubb was so grumpy. I thought she ought to be sorry for Sophia. It must be terrible to have to leave home for three weeks.

"Nonsense, she'll be as hard as nails."

At last when all was ready, even the supper table laid, I managed to get away. I had to make a last effort to see my people before Sophia arrived even though it was very wet outside. Everything seemed to be especially green and strong in the woods by the stream because she was coming. Each time I passed one of my favourite spots, I thought of how I would perhaps bring Sophia there.

My people did not come; I don't know why I expected them. They so dislike the rain. I left a sign that I had been, and returned home.

As soon as I opened the kitchen door I sensed that Sophia had arrived. I did not wait to remove my coat,

I could not. I ran upstairs and knocked on her bedroom door.

She is beautiful, my cousin. She was seated on the bed with one hand lying on my cushion, wearing the softest pink dress, low-waisted and trimmed with ribbons and broderie anglaise. She has dark, dark hair which rested thickly on her shoulders, and on her feet she wore tiny, neat strap shoes. She smiled at me, rose very gracefully and gave me her hand.

I don't know what I said. I was too nervous and felt awkward standing there with my wet hair. She was thoughtful, like an adult. She told me to go and dry myself. I'm afraid I must have looked shabby in my dirty cotton print dress; but I cannot expect to match her expensive clothes.

At supper she was very polite, but quiet. She has a tiny appetite and merely nibbled at some toast. Mother talked mostly, asking after my uncle and aunt and poor Nicholas. She discussed measles at length and told Sophia how ill I had been with them and how I had had mumps. It made me feel silly, but Sophia didn't mind at all, and answered everything with great charm.

She seemed very tired and went to bed soon after the meal. She did not get up until ten this morning. Mrs Bubb wanted me to go and call her in time for breakfast, but mother gave me some tea to take to her instead. Sophia has the most beautiful nightgown with rows of lace in the neck and sleeves.

It has rained all day. I took Sophia up to my room this morning and suggested she might like to look at my books and dolls. She did not seem interested in them. Of course she is too old for dolls. I am really. Also, none of my old toys is in very good condition.

I hope Sophia will not find it too quiet here. I wish the sun would shine. She asked me what I normally do on wet days during the holidays.

"Oh I practise the piano, or help Mrs Bubb and mother, or read, or play, or study." I could not tell her about my dreams, or my private games, or my people. I may never tell her.

"What about you?" I asked.

"I would not even get up until midday," she said, rather impatiently. "And then there'd be callers, or flowers to arrange, or embroidery of course. Usually my brother and I go to stay with my Uncle Thomas for the summer season. He has a house on the coast."

I don't know much about Sophia's Uncle Thomas because he's on her father's side. I asked her why she had not gone to stay with him this time.

"Good gracious, I might be infectious!" she exclaimed. "It's all right to come here, you've had the measles."

She has gone to bed early again tonight.

I pray that the sun might shine tomorrow so I can take her in the garden and to the village. I expect she seems unhappy at the moment because she is homesick and still tired after the journey. I hope she will settle down. I like her so much. I just hope I don't seem too childish and silly to her.

It was a mistake to think she'd be interested in dolls.

Tuesday, 20 July

Yesterday was warm and breezy and the sun shone. I took Sophia on a tour of Needlewick. I did not go near the Tunnels or my people, of course. I still feel very nervous and shy of her. She's so much more experienced than I am; our lives up until now have been so different it is hard to believe we are cousins and share the same grandparents.

We went along the lane to the village. There were still puddles from Sunday's rain and they gleamed. I walked in all the muddy bits with my thick boots so that Sophia wouldn't damage her thin shoes. Everything was very rich and bloomy. Sophia was surprised by all the butterflies — small white ones mostly. By the river near the Cheltenham road there is a mass of meadowsweet; the breeze wafted its ripe, grainy scent towards us. I love touching the cool, fluffy heads of the flowers. Sophia says wild flowers make her sneeze.

We met Michael by the river. He was lying on the bank spitting into the water. I called to him and introduced him to Sophia. He stood with his hands in his pockets, his head down, gazing at his feet.

"This is Michael, he helps father," I told Sophia.

"Good morning, Michael," she said in her smooth, cool voice.

He twisted his neck sideways and squinted up at her. He then proceeded to stare at her until we left. As we walked on towards the bridge, I glanced round and saw that he was still gazing after us.

Sophia said: "Helen, are you on such familiar terms with all the servants in Needlewick?"

"But he's father's page," I said.

"Page! Isn't that rather a grand title for an errand boy?"

"Well, I suppose so. He does other jobs though. I suppose he's not a real page. We just call him that. He likes it."

She seemed astonished. I felt a bit ashamed.

At the bridge I suggested we had races with sticks.

"What on earth do you mean?" she asked.

"You know, we each choose a stick, drop it in the water and then run to the other side of the bridge to see whose appears first."

"What's the point?" she demanded.

I keep forgetting that because she's a year older than me she doesn't want to play childish games.

She was very quiet all the time. I asked her if anything

was wrong. She said she was just concentrating on keeping her skirts clean.

I don't think she found much to interest her in Needlewick. She said she thought it was a cramped, dirty village and that it was a shame improvements weren't made on the cottages along the river to make them more picturesque. Apparently the inhabitants of Chelney village, which is near Chelney House, her parents' country home in Hertfordshire, all have beautiful cottages. We called at the shop for raspberry drops but she wouldn't eat any because she said they hurt her teeth. I told her about the old inn, but apparently my father has already given its history. I began to think she was bored with me and suggested that we might visit Mrs Gresham. Sophia said she was too tired.

Mother had given me some strawberry jam for the Makepeace family so we had to call on them. "They are very poor," I told Sophia. "I'm afraid Mr Makepeace does not support them adequately."

"Why ever not?"

"I believe he drinks too much."

She looked disgusted. "They should stop him," she said firmly.

However, when I suggested that she might like to wait outside the cottage she refused. I admire her for going in with me. All the girls were there, as well as Mrs Makepeace who is very large again. Sophia says such matters as pregnancy are not spoken of in polite circles. I wonder how the topic is avoided. Mrs Makepeace always makes me horribly awkward and I felt very foolish standing in the middle of the crowded kitchen with Sophia and a pot of jam. Through an open door I could see into the bedroom with its untidy row of mattresses. Being in the Makepeace house always fills me with horror. Mother says I must not get too close to the children because the insects which crawl from their hair are catching.

But the Makepeace children never look particularly miserable. There are some far poorer children in the village, although they are the biggest family. It is Mrs Makepeace who always seems so tired and ill-fed. She is so wrapped up in herself, and remote. Perhaps that's why I don't like her. She wears an old grey striped dress which I believe is a cast-off from one of the servants up at Middlecote Hall. She has very large eyes, too large, and she doesn't seem to need to blink much. She frightens me with those staring eyes. I was glad Mr Makepeace wasn't there. I dread to think what Sophia would make of him.

I introduced Sophia to Mrs Makepeace.

"This is my cousin from London. She has come to stay while her brother recovers from measles."

She shook Sophia's hand. She likes touching people.

"I hope you're not infectious. I don't want this lot going down with anything."

Sophia laughed. "I think I would have felt ill by now if I was going to have measles."

She was very kind to Mrs Makepeace and asked the names of all the girls. We gave the children our sweets. I could see they were greatly in awe of Sophia. She did look very beautiful in a blue dress with a tiny white collar and her hair all loose and shiny beneath her hat. I felt that I really liked her as I watched her with those children. I think that, if she is so sympathetic, so quick to respond to children, she will understand about my people. I'd love to tell her so she could visit them with me. Then she wouldn't be bored. Then she'd be really interested in me.

After we had left the Makepeace house, Sophia said she needed some fresh air so I suggested we walk up to the church and over the hill home. It was so warm and sunny we were able to sit in the meadow near the river where the Middlecote donkey is sometimes tethered. The grass is quite short there and felt dry. I picked daisies and showed Sophia how to make a chain. I asked her many questions, wanting to hear about London, and my Aunt Suzanna, and Nicholas.

Sophia always looks so dreamy when she talks about her mama. She sat in the grass with her ankles crossed, her large hat tipped over her eyes to shade her face. She has wonderful dark eyes, but she says she hates her complexion. She says she'd rather have pink and white skin like mine. I've never thought of my skin as being pink and white before. She says I should wear a larger hat to protect my nose.

She told me about the country house-parties which her parents frequently attend. Her mother takes three trunks full of clothes.

"Just for three days?" I asked.

"Of course. She could never wear the same thing twice. In the morning she must change from, for instance, a walking or riding ensemble into something suitable for lunch. Then she wears an afternoon dress and later a tea gown, and finally, of course there're her evening gowns."

"What are her dresses like?"

"Oh Helen, she has so many."

"Well, describe your favourite."

"My favourite is pink and begins here." She pointed to the middle of her chest.

"No!"

"Yes, and it makes her waist look as tiny as this." She held her hands in a small circle.

"What do they do all day?"

"Oh they talk, and eat, and sometimes it takes mama an hour to change from one gown to another because of course her hair must be re-dressed." I worked out that Aunt Suzanna must spend four hours a day dressing. "Sometimes they play croquet or tennis. Mama is an expert tennis player. But of course it's the meals that take up the time."

"Why?"

"Well, it takes your family an hour to eat two courses. Imagine how long eight would take."

I cannot imagine a meal with eight courses. How could anyone eat that much?

"And they drink different wine with nearly every course. And then they dance or play cards."

"We play cards," I said.

"For money?"

I don't think she likes being interrupted.

She suddenly gave me a very odd sideways look.

"And then of course there's love."

"What do you mean?"

"Well for instance, mama's bedroom is always near Sir Richard Welsh's room."

"Why?"

She gave me that odd look again, as if to see whether or not I would be shocked.

"Richard is in love with my mother. He dances with her whenever he can. They are always together. And hostesses always put their rooms next to each other."

"What about your father, doesn't he mind?"

"Oh no. He encourages it. He likes mama to have titled friends. He and mama give parties too, at Chelney. Nicholas and I are allowed to appear there sometimes. I love that."

"And what do you do while your parents are away?"

"I stay in London with the servants. I have a companion called Miss Pinner."

"I should miss mother dreadfully if she went away like that."

"Oh, one gets used to it."

I should never like it. Mother went away once for a week after she had been ill. I hated it. The house was very lonely. Father was out such a lot on calls, and Mrs Bubb seemed to be continually in a temper.

"Why is your father so rich?" I asked. I hope it wasn't too rude.

"He's a financier. He deals with money and business. He's getting richer all the time. He's very concerned that he and mama should mix with the best people so that they can have good social standing. You see it's difficult to be accepted in the very best houses if you're not from a good family."

I wondered what she meant.

Sophia continued: "Of course, it's marvellous for me. By the time I come out, I shall have immediate access to all the best circles. Father hopes I shall make a brilliant marriage."

I think of Roundstones with its smooth white walls and black painted window frames. It's quite small, I suppose, but so comfortable. My father is sometimes rather abrupt in his manner, but he loves mother and me. He cares for the Makepeace family and others like them. That's what's important to him. And mother only has five or six dresses, but she doesn't mind. She likes cooking and visiting. She is very happy. And I can't imagine her having a lover. What an extraordinary thing! My uncle seems to accept this Sir Richard Welsh — he actually encourages his wife. Perhaps he doesn't love Aunt Suzanna as much as my father loves mother.

Sophia has told me so much about her family — so much that is private. She has honoured me by confiding in me. Someday, when I have the courage, and am sure of her, I shall return these confidences.

In the meantime, I must continue to find ways to prevent her getting homesick. She often sighs and looks very sad. I know that I am not very good company at times. Mother tells me that I'm a terrible dreamer and sometimes seem to be in a world no one else can get through to. I must try harder to entertain my cousin. I hope she does not feel that I do not care for her.

Saturday, 24 July
My mind is made up. Tomorrow I shall talk to Sophia about my people. She keeps telling me things, giving me books, sharing her feelings with me. I feel so dull sometimes, unable to contribute anything of interest to our conversations. I must repay her with something. I hope she will understand. Will she laugh at me? A little at first perhaps, but not when she has been to the Tunnel Woods.

I am afraid that once she has left Needlewick she will forget me, and I shall lose her. It is so lovely to have a real companion. I am very jealous when she talks to me about Nicholas. I feel shut out from their friendship which is silly of me. How could I have expected to be a part of their lives before now? I'd love to have had a brother. Nicholas sounds such fun. Sophia misses him so much. If I show her my people, she will know that I, too, have someone really special to love.

I cannot wait to see her face when I tell her about them. I have kept my knowledge of them to myself for so long. And of course, once I have told her, I shall be able to visit them again. I have missed them so much during the past week, but I have never really been able to get away. Sophia would think it strange if I left her alone for a whole afternoon.

So I am determined. Tomorrow, after lunch, I shall take her to the river, and we'll lie on the smooth ground under the willow, and I'll tell her. I am very nervous and excited. If she laughs at me I shall be very hurt, for the sake of my people who are so easily offended. And I know they have always warned me against telling my secret to anyone, but that was before I knew Sophia. I'm sure when they meet her they will understand.

Besides, Sophia is very worried at the moment and needs a distraction. Apart from missing her home she is very concerned about her mama. Nicholas has written at last and says his mother is very unhappy.

It seems that Sir Richard has quarrelled with Aunt Suzanna. I think that this can only be a good thing, surely. It can hardly be right for a married woman to have a lover. In my imagination, Aunt Suzanna wears one of those beautiful low-cut gowns and a swansdown boa that Sophia has often told me about, and stands beside Sir Richard, who is tall and dark and wears a black evening suit. Aunt Suzanna turns away her head to hide her tears.

But how could Sophia's papa allow them to have become such close friends? Sophia says little about her father except that he is quiet and busy and rarely speaks to her. Well my father is very busy, but he always has time for me. He sits me on his knee in the leather chair by the study fire, even though mother says that I should behave more like a grown-up girl. I love him to tell me little stories about his patients. Sophia's papa sounds frightening. I think he must be a lonely man who would actually like to be his wife's lover himself. Can social position really be so important to him?

I know Sophia is very unhappy about her mama and thinks about her constantly. She says her mother is rarely upset like this. Perhaps soon she will be happy with Uncle Simon again, but Sophia says this is impossible.

Apart from Sophia's unhappiness, which I would dearly like to help, it has been a good week, because I enjoy Sophia's company so much.

She makes me laugh almost hysterically at times. Apparently her mother and her friends have their own way of speaking, and Sophia often uses it without thinking.

"Helen!" she cries. "Don't you think this dress is absolutely deevy?" This means "divine".

She was referring to a beautifully delicate lawn dress she wore to the garden party this afternoon. It was trimmed with yards of creamy lace and decorated in tiny brown and yellow flowers.

She and I walked ahead of my parents down the meadow to the footbridge and up the path to the Middlecotes' house. Sophia seemed much happier this afternoon. She is always more cheerful when she is looking her best in one of her most attractive dresses. I asked her to tell me some more funny words and she pranced along, quite undignified for her, exclaiming: "Oh Helen, I do think your black shoes are delicatissimo. And don't you think that crop of buttercups is quite superbare?"

I tried to join in, but somehow the words sounded awkward and ridiculous from my lips.

"No, no, Helen, carissimo!" shrieked Sophia. "Not like that. You have to trill the wordares lightly. How long will it take up to reach the gardenare?"

It doesn't seem funny at all now, but I laughed so much then that mother kept asking us to share the joke.

All the stalls were spread out behind Middlecote Hall on the lawn which leads to the little bank and then the rougher ground beyond, where the daffodils grow in the spring. From a distance we could hear music and a subdued murmur of voices. The lawn, with all those figures followed by their black, squat shadows looked brilliantly green and lit. Bunting had been tied to each stall and from tree to tree. The big white marquee for the tea billowed and flapped in the breeze. The garden party at Middlecote Hall is the same every year, and I always love it. It means summer; the drifting sound of voices in the open air; the summer clothes, summer flowers; the band; the smell of trodden grass.

Sophia was so excited. She gave everyone she met a friendly smile. She talked to all the Makepeace children, and bought all six toffee apples.

Sophia was extra nice to Mrs Gresham. "How lovely to see you!" she exclaimed. "You're looking absolutely wonderful, Mrs Gresham." It seemed natural for Sophia to be addressing her as one adult to another. I wish I could adopt that breezy way of talking to people which seems to come naturally to Sophia.

We spoke for a while to Sir George. He teased us by saying we should not be talking to an old chap like him when there were so many young men longing to catch a glimpse of us.

The garden party was altogether a great success. The sun shone very hot, and the tea tent was like an oven. But I love the hot smell of canvas and damp grass and the way everyone drifts around sipping at cups of tea. The women all wore their best hats. Sophia says many of them are out of date, but she agreed that for Needle-wick they all looked very smart.

I won a coconut. I don't like coconuts so I gave it to Mrs Bubb. Mother bought a little crocheted mat for the hall stand. She suggested Sophia might like to buy one for her mama, but Sophia said her mother had hundreds of little mats, and anyway such fancy items were not entirely fashionable. I believe Mrs Granger who was running the stall was rather upset. She is doubtless ignorant of the kind of circles that Sophia moves in whilst in London.

Towards the end of the afternoon, Sir George made a speech that I could not quite understand. I heard father whisper that George had been in the beer tent far too long. Usually I am asked to pick out the prize winners of the draw, but this year Sophia volunteered, and everyone clapped as she presented the prizes.

Our Michael won some scent. He is an odd boy. He lay in wait for us on the way home. Mother and father were walking ahead and he suddenly appeared beside Sophia and held out the bottle.

"You can have it," he said.

"Oh, thank you!" she replied gravely. She undid the top and sniffed. "Cheap rubbish," she murmured to me. It did smell rather over-sweet but I hope Michael didn't hear. He wouldn't understand that she is used to expensive perfume. He has never given me anything.

I'm very tired. These gatherings always wear me out, and the sun made my head ache by the end. Sophia was also tired by this evening, and has been quiet since supper.

I feel very pent-up about tomorrow. I scarcely know how I shall get through the time until after lunch when we will be under the willow and I shall be telling her my secret.

Wednesday, 28 July

My people are angry with me. They say I should never have told Sophia about them — she will laugh at me and destroy the friendship I have with them. They tell me I am a fool. They say it is vanity which caused me to tell Sophia about them — I needed to boast, to prove I was special.

I am so sad I can scarcely move my pen to write. I am crippled by sadness. It hurts me to move at all. What have I done? I feel innocent of vanity. I only wanted to share with Sophia because I love her and because she has confided so much in me.

I wish Sophia had not come. I love her, but I blame her for my peoples' anger. But that's wrong. If it is anyone's fault it is mine for misunderstanding things, or theirs for not listening to me.

Today was a sky blue pink day. I lay in my bed and watched a brilliant strip of sunlight pierce the gap between the curtains. I felt warm with excitement. I wish I could return to this morning and be happy again.

I thought I was doing right. Sophia is different from anyone else — she is my cousin, and in the past couple of weeks has become like a sister to me. I trust her. How could I keep this huge secret from her when she has told me so candidly such a lot about her family?

But my people are strange. I don't think they know what love is. That is why they don't understand.

At first Sophia seemed excited about going to the Tunnel Woods. It was very breezy. The wind kept lifting her hair from her shoulders, and the cow parsley along the meadow path made her sneeze. Everything seemed to me to ripple and sway in expectation. The fresh green of the birch trees along the stream rustled and made me feel even more gloriously happy. Sophia laughed at me for racing ahead and then running back to her so that she would not be left behind.

She was tired by the time we reached the Tunnel Woods. I suppose it is a long walk, but she made it worse by wandering along so slowly. I almost became irritated with her. I am so used to that path now I never think about distance. And it's so wonderful in the valley. On one side is the stream which is clear and lively at the moment because of all the rain we had before Sophia came. At some points there are wide stepping stones. I danced about on these, hopping from one to another, trying to make Sophia join me, but she was afraid of splashing her dress. To the left of the river there is first a thin coppice and then the trees disappear and there are open fields and the path is slightly banked up beside the stream to prevent flooding. The meadows are full of flowers at this time of year; masses of buttercups and tansy. Then, when the path plunges into a copse there is a hint of how the shadows will be in the Tunnel Woods. After that there is a stretch of ripening corn, and then, at last, the Tunnel Woods.

I was so excited that I wanted to carry straight on until I reached my people, but Sophia said she was tired and hungry and needed to rest to regain her strength before we entered the woods. So we sat by the stream and ate our tea and I stripped off my stockings and dabbled my hot toes. The water was so cold it made my feet ache. Sophia said my ankles would turn brown if I exposed them to sunlight. I suppose they are a little brown already, but nobody sees them except me, and I love the feeling of grass and cold stream water on them.

Sophia was unhappy today, anyway. She has received a letter from her brother. By tea-time she was listless and miserable. She nibbled at her bread and jam, and kept swatting impatiently at flies, although I warned her this is not the way to deal with them. They were a great nuisance today — they seemed to come from miles around to buzz about us as we ate our picnic. I was not stung, but Sophia seemed to be particularly attractive to them and her skin came up in great bumps. They even bit her behind the ears. She seemed so tired and annoyed I suggested that perhaps we should visit my people on some other occasion — I wanted them to meet her when she was in a good mood. But she said: "I've come so far; I might as well not give up now."

I said: "I'm sorry, Sophia."

She smiled at me then and replied: "Nonsense, the heat has given me a headache, that's all."

As we entered the Tunnel Woods, I felt the cool shade cloak me in soft, dappled browns. The wood was quiet and sleepy in the afternoon sun and smelt sweet. The nettles along the path grow very strong because no-one ever goes that way except me. They seemed to be even thicker today. I suppose, because I was worried about

Sophia, the path seemed to be full of obstacles. She kept brushing her hands against the stinging nettles. I found her a dock-leaf but she threw it away saying it was dirty.

At last we began to climb away from the brook. The path there is steep, but I usually enjoy that part of the journey so much because there are so many surprises along the way. Suddenly there's a tiny clearing where the sun throbs warm on lush grass or I come across a little pool of dark water with flies skipping over its surface. Or I might notice especially the enormous bulging trunk of an oak tree, or the soft curve of a bank of dead leaves. And all the time I am becoming more excited because I know I am nearly with my people. And so I love climbing up the muddy path, criss-crossed by roots which act as steps, each step taking me nearer. But every time we came to a particularly steep part today, I thought of Sophia and how tired she already was. She was perspiring a good deal. Her face was wet.

At the Tunnels she stopped.

"I can't go in there," she whispered.

"Why not?"

"It's so dark; I can't see the end."

I had never thought of the Tunnels as being frightening, even on the day I first found them. "Don't worry," I told her. "Hold my hand."

She tugged against me all the way along, her nails digging into my palm. I had to pull her up the pile of rubble between the two sections of Tunnel because she was afraid of falling.

"It's not far at all now," I said encouragingly. "This is the exciting bit, where the bracken grows above your head."

But she said she didn't like bracken because it smells so sour. I could hear her feet kicking at stalks as she trudged behind me. Even in the bracken it was very hot.

In the clearing the breeze stirred the soft tufty grass and the leaves of the surrounding trees. The air was sweet and woody. I had no sense that my people were there. We wandered all round. At last I made Sophia sit at the edge of the clearing and I went to the hawthorn. I laid my cheek against its rough bark and waited.

Sophia sat very still. I could feel her watching me intently. Suddenly I felt foolish. How odd she must have thought me. She must have wondered at me leaning there against the hawthorn tree. But I still waited, even though I've never had quite that feeling of shame and awkwardness before. It was cool in the shade of the hawthorn tree, with the wind ruffling the branches. Finally I forgot all about Sophia. In my hands were the dry leaves, crisped and warmed by the sun.

There was anger.

Such anger.

It burned my lips and cheeks and thrust my head back into the tree. I was dazed by their anger.

I said: "I've brought my cousin."

But only their rage replied and tore at the grasses and the blue sky.

How, how had I done wrong? How had I betrayed them? Every blade of grass stood on its own, separate, and the clearing was silent. I had been chosen. And I had been chosen because I was alone.

But now I have someone and she is precious to me. When I touch her hand I feel her warm skin. Her hair is silk and she lets me comb it. She is full of life and knowledge. She gives and gives for no reason but that she loves me.

I have nothing to give in return but the clearing. Isn't it mine to give?

Laughter then, but not kind.

Sophia was standing beside me, her face white, her eyes fixed on my face.

I was crying.

She took my hand. "What happened?" she asked.

"You saw what happened."

"Saw? I saw nothing. Only you."

"Yes, they're gone now."

"But Helen, who are gone?"

"My people."

"Oh Helen, you don't need to pretend to me. I understand. But don't pretend."

I gazed at her, astonished. "They were here, Sophia." Then I saw the look on her face. "You don't believe me at all, do you?"

She smiled. "Look, I'm awfully tired. Can't we go home?"

"Yes, we'll go the quick way they showed me."

I walked to where I thought the short-cut path wound away through the trees. I became anxious when I realised I could not find it. Surely it couldn't have grown over in the two weeks since I'd last been there?

"Now what are you doing?" Sophia demanded.

"I'm looking for the path, it's a quicker way back along the top of the valley."

But I could find no path out of the clearing except the one which led back through the Tunnels. The sun was blazing down on us still. I was drained of energy.

"Oh for heaven's sake, Helen, do pull yourself together. The other path must be here if you've used it before."

But we could not find that path. We had no choice but to trail home by the stream. We walked almost in silence. Sophia wouldn't reply if I said something and soon I felt too miserable to speak.

When we at last arrived home, she ran straight up to her room and slammed the door. I went and lay down on my bed. I feel a little better now I have written all this down, but only a little. What should I do? I can't sleep. I keep thinking of Sophia's sulky face, of the Tunnels and the hawthorn tree which gave no protection.

There is one more thing. Nicholas's letter. I feel sick about that too. Usually Sophia reads her letters alone and then comes to find me and tell me all about the amusing things which have been happening in London. But yesterday she took her letter away and did not return. Eventually I went to find her.

"Are you all right?" I asked. I sat beside her and took her hand. It felt cold.

"How can I tell you," she replied, "after all the things I've said? How can I tell you how unhappy everything is?"

"What do you mean?"

She was silent for a long time. Then she gave a deep sigh. "You won't understand, but I'll tell you. I have to tell you. I have been lying to you. What do you know about my papa?"

"I know he's very rich. I know I do not understand him." I was thinking of how he had allowed his wife to become so friendly with another man.

"Papa is a terrible man. He's cold. I hate him. He's cold and cruel. He laughs at me. He laughs at mama. He gives her presents: jewels, money, gowns, and then laughs at her for enjoying them. He goes to parties and to country houses, and all the time he sneers. How could you understand? You live in such a cosy little world. Your parents love each other. My papa just uses my mother. He wants to be accepted everywhere, not just rich, so he uses her loveliness to get invited to houses where he wouldn't otherwise be asked."

I have seen a wedding photograph of my uncle and aunt. She is very small and slender. Her hair is fair and tumbles softly over her forehead. Her eyes are large; her nose narrow and delicate. She has a little crease on either side of her mouth, as if made by smiling.

My uncle is tall and thin. His gazes straight ahead. He rests his hand on my aunt's shoulder.

"So what has happened now?" I whispered.

Apparently there has been a terrible argument. Nicholas heard it. He was in the library and they didn't know he was there. My uncle was in the drawing room, ready to go to a reception. Aunt Suzanna came in, still wearing her afternoon gown. She said she wouldn't go anywhere else with my uncle or with Sir Richard. She said they both used her and did not care for her at all — they just wanted something pretty to be seen with. They treated her as a toy, to be picked up and played with when they chose. She knew that she was only allowed to go around with Sir Richard because he was titled and would help them get invited to great houses. She has quarrelled with Sir Richard too — she realised that he only wanted her because she was a famous beauty.

My uncle became very angry. He listed all he had done for her in the past, how much she had cost him. He commanded her to go out with him and when she refused he strode over, seized her shoulders, and began hitting her across the neck and face. Nicholas interrupted. Since then my uncle and aunt have not spoken to each other. Nicholas talks only to his mother, who will see no-one but him.

When Sophia told me all this I started to shiver. I believe I cried out when she said how her mother had been beaten. I have seen a drunkard in the village strike his wife. I cannot imagine someone like my uncle hitting a woman.

Sophia says I must tell no-one about this. Her mother told Nicholas he mustn't write to her about it, but he felt he had to.

Sometimes life seems so sad. I was so much happier when I began writing this diary. Now I no longer feel sure of my people. And I keep worrying about Aunt Suzanna. He might hit her again.

Sunday, 1 August
I feel so much better than when I last wrote. I have seen my people again. And yesterday we all went on a marvellous picnic; the Greshams, the Middlecotes and our family, even father. The weather was not particularly kind but we had such fun.

I went alone to visit my people on Friday. I had a delicious walk to the Tunnel Woods. A strong breeze blew but it was quite warm. Warm air swept about my face and legs — I felt beautiful as I dashed along the path. The sunlight shone on the river. I love staring up into the great trees and seeing the clear blue gleaming between the shining leaves. And I love the solid brownness of the tree trunks.

But I did not feel quite as carefree as I usually do when I go to the clearing. I was anxious about what would happen there.

It is odd. On Friday the Tunnels frightened me. I have never been afraid of them before. But they seemed so dark and long, and I kept remembering Sophia's fear of them. But eventually I came through safely and hurried to the clearing. There was no one about. I sat on the soft grass and gazed up at the sky. Tiny clouds were racing above the clearing. Everything was heavy and rustling. The sun was warm on my face.

Of course they came.

The leaves whispered, the hawthorn stirred and the grasses were bright in the sunlight. All around the woods were great with wind. I thought they had changed, but they said it was I who had changed.

My eyes, they said, had grown old.

How can eyes grow old?

There was no reply.

Next time, shall I bring Sophia?

Bring her, bring her, what does it matter?

Will she see you, will she?

Bring her, bring her.

They came, and the breeze was soft on my cheeks. Lovely breeze, and soft, singing leaves.

When it was time to leave I found the other way out of the woods with no difficulty.

As I walked home I did feel better. I have not lost them. I found the other path. I will bring Sophia again and then she'll see. Oh, is it greedy to want both? I don't think so.

I trod so easily, as if walking were no effort at all. I looked across the valley and loved Middlecote Hall, its square, large-windowed walls all honey-coloured, bathed in rich, afternoon sunshine. I waved at the tiny figure of a man in the field above. He stood with his shadow stretched out clearer than himself. He did not see me. I do not know who it was.

I love the old elms I pass on my way home by the short-cut path they showed me. They stand in a group of three on the edge of a field, bending slightly together, huge and graceful and very strong, their roots banking up the soil. When I look at the elm trees everything seems to be firm and pure and everlasting.

Yesterday was the picnic. Unfortunately the weather had broken and it was a grey, damp day and the wind blew more strongly than ever. It was a wild day.

The Greshams bicycled to Stonyfort Hill where we were to meet. The rest of us drove. Sophia wore a bright sprigged dress with a broad sash. I wondered whether she'd be warm enough. Mother had made me wear my brown wool dress though the sleeves are too tight. She said we would be very chilly and exposed on the hill.

The wind whipped and tore at the hedgerows and blew dust up in the lane. My father seemed to be in good spirits and talked to the horses in such a comical way I couldn't stop giggling.

The picnic was hilarious. The Greshams had arrived first and Mrs Gresham had a table-cloth wrapped round her — she kept trying to lay it flat against the wind. She made my mother and Lady M, Sophia and me each sit on a corner until it was weighed down by food. We all said how ridiculous it was to have a picnic in such weather. Sophia was cold so father wrapped her in the huge plaid blanket from the trap and said she looked like a Red Indian squaw with her dark hair and skin and the blanket.

She sat huddled up while Mrs Gresham asked her about her mother. I felt dreadfully sorry for Sophia as she said brightly: "Oh dear mama is wonderfully well. I hear from her and my brother regularly. We are such a close-knit little family, you know."

She is so brave, covering her sadness like this. Mrs Gresham said, a little coolly, and almost as if she were laughing at Sophia: "How very fortunate for you all."

Sophia said dreamily: "I miss them all dreadfully."

"I expect you do," said Lady Middlecote sympathetically, "but at least here you have Helen, who must be like a sister to you."

"Yes," Sophia replied, "what more could I ask? I have Helen."

There was something in the way she spoke which made me feel suddenly terribly unhappy.

I think Mrs Gresham must have sensed it for she got up suddenly and asked me if I'd like a go on her bicycle.

I stood up slowly. I seemed to ache a little from being so long on the grass. But riding the bicycle was so exciting. I've done it quite often before, but I always feel terrified at first. But then Mr Gresham came and took hold of the cycle and I felt much safer. He ran down the track beside me with his hand on the saddle and I loved the feel of speed and the wind on my face and hair.

Poor Mr Gresham was soon red and panting. We staggered back up the hill with the bicycle between us. At the top he laid it against a tree and put one arm round me and the other round his wife who'd waited there, and we went back to the picnic. Father and Sir George were smoking and mother and Lady M were holding on to their hats and chatting about the forthcoming wedding of Lady M's niece, Catherine. We are all invited as mother and Mrs Gresham knew Lady Middlecote and her sister so well when they were all little girls together.

Sophia was sitting apart from the others, reading a book her brother had sent her. I know it's silly but I sometimes feel a bit jealous when she is reading. She gets so involved and scarcely seems aware of what's happening around her. Her current book is called *Audrey* and is about a girl whose entire family is killed by an Indian tribe.

I sat beside her, thinking she might be feeling a little lonely. She turned to me at once and held my hand.

"Cousin Helen," she said.

We have a great joke of calling each other cousin. She has never touched me like that before. I keep looking at my hand, and remembering that moment.

"Do you mind if I sit here? Will I disturb you?" I asked.

"Of course not. You know there is no one else I'd rather be with."

I turned my head so she would not see my tears.

*

Thursday, 5 August

It has been so hot this week I have not felt like writing. It's difficult to sleep. However, although we have been complaining about the heat, we hope the weather will hold for Saturday. I am so excited. I've only been to one wedding before and that was when I was four so I can scarcely remember it. Sophia says she has been to several, so I expect this country wedding won't seem very grand to her. It is lovely to have Sophia here, so that I can share all my excitement.

Mother has been refurbishing my best primrose yellow dress. She has added new ruffles to the neck and hem in white lace, and Lady Middlecote has given me some scraps of white swansdown which is fearfully expensive. I thought the result was quite beautiful. Sophia said: "Yes, it's lovely but when you come to choose your own dresses I suggest strong colours and much plainer styles. But of course that's magnifico — so summery and ideal for a wedding."

She has a white dress with a chiffon overskirt and the most dainty green embroidery. I told her she looked like a Kate Greenaway picture, and she said: "Good heavens, I'm not pretty in the least."

"No," I replied, and then murmured very softly: "No Sophia, you are not pretty, you are beautiful."

She smoothed her hair which always hangs in a shining mass straight across her back, and looked pleased. "Ah, if you could see my mother and her friends you would not say that."

My mother has a delightful new hat in pink and blue.

I'm longing to see the bride and her dress. Sophia has pattern books and magazines and a Harrods catalogue her brother sent her and we spend hours browsing through them. She says the only person in Needlewick who is truly elegantly dressed is Mrs Gresham. I didn't mention that Mrs Gresham makes most of her own clothes.

We went to tea with Mrs Gresham — I don't think Sophia liked it there much. I love the garden; there is a high wall all round and a little gate leads under an arch and on to a flagged path up to the front door. The whole garden is full of mysteries. Little higgledy-piggledy paths run along the grass dividing the garden into shrubbery, kitchen garden and a sweet hedged area full of roses and with a little pond. We sat in this part of the garden under a tree and sipped tea. Sophia says she does not like sitting under trees because you never know what might fall on your head.

The trouble is that Mrs Gresham always asks after Aunt Suzanna. Poor Sophia has to be so reserved — it must be a strain answering these questions.

Yesterday Mrs Gresham began: "How is your mother, Sophia?"

"She's very well."

"You always say that. I wish you could give me more news of her. She hasn't written to me for many months now. She and your aunt and I used to be so close."

Sophia replied, "Oh, I don't hear from her very often myself."

"Your brother writes frequently though, doesn't he, Sophia? He's so much better now," I said, hoping to change the subject.

"Oh yes. He keeps me in touch."

"I expect your mother is too busy going to parties to spend much time writing to you, Sophia," Mrs Gresham suggested. Her voice sounded unusually harsh and unkind.

Sophia became a little angry. She loves her mother so much.

"My mother has not been to a party for a fortnight as

far as I know. She's been going to meetings. She is a very serious person."

I wondered what she meant. The last Sophia had told me about her mama was that she was keeping to her room and was desperately unhappy.

"What kind of meetings?"

"With other women," replied Sophia, toying with a crumb of bread and butter.

Mrs Gresham was sitting with her hands folded in her lap, her fair head slightly on one side. She looked quite young with the sunlight behind her. "I must write to Suzanna," she said softly. Then we helped to clear the tea and we spoke of other things.

I cannot think for long about anything except the wedding at the moment. And tomorrow I'm going to take Sophia to the clearing again. I do hope they will be kind to her. Oh my life is so good and full!

Sunday, 8 August
The last few days have been so dreadful. Is it always the case that something you've really looked forward to will be a disappointment? Sophia says it is best never to look forward to anything and then nice things can only be a pleasant surprise.

I took her to see my people on Friday. I cannot think of them at the moment except with distaste. Cruel games, they play. They hate Sophia.

And then on the way home it was so hot I was dizzy and faint. And all the way I felt as if we were being followed, which is stupid because I know no-one goes to those woods except me, and certainly no-one else knows the other way home. And Sophia irritated me because she kept asking me questions. She does not understand at all.

And yesterday the wedding, instead of being the

joyful event I had expected, was awful. Either the heat or the motion of the carriage which had no opening window unsettled me but I felt quite ill. My head was heavy and hot. I hardly dared eat all day because of the journey home.

And then a terrible storm blew up. I felt so afraid — I don't know Hippingdean at all and it seemed so dark there. The church was oppressively dim. I could not concentrate on the service. I have a vague memory of a misty white gown, of the bridesmaids in lavender and of the organ crashing. I felt cold and a hot rushing feeling kept coming to my head. I wished I was back at Roundstones in the kitchen with Mrs Bubb. The kitchen is always so comforting on bad days.

I felt lonely at the reception and quite unable to eat. Sophia was busy talking to some friends. It was nice to see her meet some people she knew. I believe she must have missed her London acquaintances so much since she's been at Roundstones. Mother, of course, talked mostly with Lady Middlecote and her sister and they discussed the other guests and the wedding or greeted old friends, and father was with the men. I sat on my own most of the time on a hard stool. It is so unlike me to feel unhappy and out of sorts in such a gathering. Usually I love to watch everyone and to hold my secret about my own friends, my people, very close. Then later I can tell them all about it.

But on Saturday I felt as if a pane of glass stood between me and the other guests. I could see them, but could not reach them. I saw the laughing, talking, eating mouths; the full, colourful skirts of the ladies; the black, sober legs of the men; the clutter of furniture and the expensive red and blue flowered carpet; the great dining-room table covered with presents; silver candlesticks, huge tureens, dainty figurines; but all the time I seemed to hear only the storm in my ears. And when I reached inside my head for my people as I usually do when I feel lonely I could not find them, or properly remember them. I was so pleased when mother at last told me it was time to leave and, yet, as we prepared to go, I felt upset, as if I had lost something very important.

Sophia kissed lots of people goodbye and seemed bright and glowing. She has mixed with so many people and attended so many grand functions. I wish I had a little more experience of the world. I feel as if I've been dreadfully shut away in Needlewick. Mother is the same. How can she teach me about life when she has hardly ventured beyond Needlewick herself? How unlike her sister she is. Aunt Suzanna has done and seen so much more, simply because she married a rich man, and mother only a country doctor. Sophia says I may go and stay with her in London one day, but what would I find to talk about? Anyway, Sophia's home seems such a muddle these days. I do not understand Aunt Suzanna at all. How can she give up her beautiful life to attend dreadful meetings which her husband doesn't approve of — for this is what Sophia says is happening.

No, I'm afraid I would feel fearfully in the way — or "de trop" as Sophia says — were I to go and stay with her. But then Needlewick, and Roundstones in particular, seem so dull now. I sit at table and hear father suck on his spoon as he eats soup. And mother chatters on and on about such dull topics. Do you know Sophia has even been to a Coronation? Oh, what I would have given to have been there and seen Queen Alexandra in her bell-skirted white dress and ermine-trimmed cloak! Sophia remembers the star the Queen wore at her breast flashing in the sunlight.

Sophia has seen so much in her fourteen years. I feel as if I have done nothing. Life for me has been wasted so far.

It is so stupid to cry. I feel such an odd mixture of worry and loneliness tonight.

There is one last thing about which I must write. I want to confess it and hope that, having written it, it will go away.

I am jealous of Sophia.

I had not realised it before, but when I watched her, so beautiful with the gaslamps reflected in her hair at the reception on Saturday, surrounded by admiring people, I felt envious. She has everything, I nothing. She has beauty and charm, talks easily, has many friends, wealth, even a brother, and her family owns two great houses. And I? I have nothing. I don't even think I have Sophia's love as I once believed. I suppose other people who were at the reception on Saturday were so much more interesting than me. I know I'm dull. But I think Sophia, if she had cared for me, might have spent a little time with me when I was so lonely, sitting by myself in that crowd.

I suppose now I am suffering from self-pity. That is what father would say, I know.

Sophia has leant me a book called *Little Lord Fauntleroy*. I must read that; perhaps it will cheer me. She says it's a child's book, but that I may enjoy it. I know that in her eyes I am no more than a child.

Wednesday, 11 August
Everything has gone. I shall never see my people again.

Yesterday I lay in my bed, pretending to be ill, thinking about what happened on Monday. How can my people come back? They were right to mistrust me — they will never again reveal themselves to me.

They saw Michael lying beneath the leaves, scheming to frighten and shock me. Or perhaps he was just interested to see how I would react. What hurts more than anything else is that he must have been following me for weeks to have known when and where to hide. He must have followed me to where I thought I could be entirely private and alone. He must have seen me with my people. What must he have thought as he sat and watched me? I feel as if my most private being has been stripped open and spat on.

But they would understand that Michael is only a child, and not quite right, and therefore not quite responsible — but Sophia, what must they have thought of her?

I am sure that she knew of Michael's scheme, probably even invented it. Why else did she accompany me to the clearing, when I know she hates that long walk and doesn't believe in my people? And why did she specifically tell me to go and sit under the tree?

She knew Michael would be there.

I cannot escape the horror. I will always remember it.

Some times are like that, there is a significance and then I don't forget. There was a significance in the way I felt when I woke, the way my dress fell over my head as I put it on, the taste of the morning tea, too strong and not quite hot enough. The weather was all wrong, all wrong, cool, breezy, damp, the summer all blown away and autumn come in the woods and by the river in yellowed grasses and the muddy path and the angry brown ripples on the water. Everything was damp, the air soaked though it wasn't raining, and I felt so heavy, my body was too heavy to walk. Fungus had grown in the roots of trees, terrible, spotted toadstools. I cried for the memory of the violets and the primroses in the spring. Come back lovely spring, lovely spring before Sophia. I am crying now. See how the ink has smeared.

Sophia *knew*.

"Why are you crying?"

"No reason.' But because then I loved her still I said, "I hated the wedding."

"Oh why?"

"I felt so lonely."

She laughed, of course. "Oh Helen, you should make more effort. You can't be lonely with all those people about."

"It's easy for you. You're used to talking to strangers."

"You must simply learn to take an interest in the other person, then you'll get on much better."

Is that all conversation is? What kind of interest does she mean?

She shouted in the Tunnels. She's always been afraid of them, she said she wanted to see if there was an echo but I know it was to deafen her fear.

The clearing was empty. No one would come, I knew that. It was too damp, too much unhappiness in me. But she told me to relax, they'd come if I went to the tree and if I left her at the edge of the clearing. I lay back against the trunk. I waited for the softness and the light inside. I closed my eyes.

There was a sound near my foot, a rustle. I opened my eyes but I knew they would not come. Yet I opened my eyes. The leaves moved. No, I knew, I knew it wasn't them.

I have always been so safe. I don't remember being much afraid.

There was a little white hand. Dirtied, bloodied.

And then in a rush, a great spurt of movement, Michael. A grin, a sneer, a gesture, and he was gone.

My breath was caught in my lungs. I could not breathe. But Sophia was laughing. First I heard her, then I saw her. She was laughing so much there were tears on her cheeks.

And then she came and put her arms round me and her hair fell across my face as she drew me close and kissed me and made little hushing noises as if to a baby. "Hush, ssh, Helen, hush. It's all right. It was only Michael. What a stupid trick!"

But I had seen her laughing.

I have repeated to my people so often that Sophia is loyal, sensitive and trustworthy. I have been reading the past entries in my diary and have realised how little I understood. Sophia, who I have described as being my supporter and friend, stood there speechless with laughter to see me like that, to see me crouched in the leaves so ridiculously.

I would not speak to her all the long way home.

She couldn't bear me to be quiet. She said: "Well, never mind, it'll be all right next time."

Then: "Would you like me to come with you again tomorrow, Helen? I don't mind."

And she asked again and again: "Are you all right now? Do you feel all right?"

Later she said: "You're far too old for this now, anyway, Helen. You've been a lonely girl, tucked away in a small village. But now you've got me, at least. I'll introduce you to people. You can visit me in London often, as I've told you." This was how she tried to comfort me.

So my people were right about her. They are right to despise her.

She is deceitful, how she must have laughed at me behind my back when I first revealed my secret to her. She is cruel, it is funny to her to see me, her cousin, who has poured out so much love for her, hurt and unhappy.

But quite apart from Sophia's deceit and Michael's trickery, I know their main reason for deserting me will be that I have been so weak myself. I was paralysed by fear, unable to move, stifled by the horror of those few moments. How can such a weak being expect favours?

I am left with a cold, bitter feeling of regret, and a great longing for Sophia's departure. After all, she is nothing. She is a doll dressed in expensive clothes and with a tongue ready with cruel witticisms. She is frightfully bored with anything that doesn't rotate round herself. The things I most admired about her mean nothing now. Her beauty is worthless to any but herself; her experience of the world has not taught her kindness, and even her precious brother, I suspect, is as cruel and lacking in understanding as she.

Instead of delighting in her company here, I now feel that she is like a great bluebottle spoiling everything she touches, and destroying my peace. I cannot help blaming her for all that has happened, not just Monday's incident. I would have enjoyed the wedding had she not been there, surrounded by admirers. She drains away the friendly, relaxed feeling of the gatherings I am used to attending with my parents and their friends, and replaces it with something almost competitive. Even the picnic was not as happy for me as picnics usually are because she was there, isolating herself. How glorious the summer promised to be before she came!

Now it seems autumn is almost here. All about me the green is faded, dusty and worn out. And what have I to look forward to now, but days of endless boredom? School for a few more terms and then many dull years at home before my possible marriage? When I had my people I felt myself to be the most blessed person on earth, now I feel the most deprived and unhappy.

I am haunted by hateful memories. I remember the storm at Hippingdean, the stillness which lay over everything on that dreadful journey, as if a hot blanket had smothered all sound. I remember how frightened I was when I first heard that slow rumble of thunder as we entered the church. At night I lie and think of those stained glass windows flickering with strips of lightning, and the damp smell of the women's wraps as they dried after being in the rain. And I remember the endless drum drum of the rain, even through all the happy noise of the reception and the dark windows so black compared to the lit rooms within.

I remember that storm and how frail it made me feel. I am so aware of my own smallness suddenly. While I had my people I was someone marked out and special, but now I am a nobody. I am precisely what I'm sure Sophia thinks I am: an ugly, unintelligent nobody. I'm not even a man. If I were, I might, just might, have got away.

It's odd, isn't it, that I don't hate Michael? He's an unlovable boy, but I can't hate him, whereas Sophia makes me almost wince with hatred when I see her now. Perhaps because I loved her so unquestioningly before.

Evening
After I had finished writing the above, I couldn't bear to be in the house any longer, so I walked into Needlewick. I had no fixed purpose. I thought perhaps I would comfort myself by doing all the things which gave me such pleasure before Sophia came. She was reading in the garden, and luckily did not press to come with me.

It is warm again. The lane was dry and the mud rough and dusty. All the flowers in the hedgerows looked as if they were dying. The cows in the meadow were lazily tossing their tails to and fro, swatting at flies. Poor things. I used to love cows, and their gentle, questioning brown eyes. Today they irritated me because they were so tranquil and accepting of their lot. I heard a skylark and that cheered me a little. I saw it winging up into the blue sky at the side of the valley. I was plagued by horse-flies.

Needlewick was half asleep, of course. A few of the Makepeace children accompanied me to the shop. It was deliciously cool and dark inside. I bought them some toffee.

Afterwards I wandered up the High Street. Usually I love Needlewick but today I felt discontented with its sameness. Nothing was happening — even if I had met someone, there would have been nothing worthwhile for us to say. Then I reached the church. I was so hot I wandered in and rested my back on one of the cold, polished benches. I like the church. It is full of mystery. It has been the same all through the years. To me it seems to be holding a breathful of vivid memories whenever I'm in there alone. It's as if, once I am gone, the church will breathe out, and all the people who have cried, or wed, or been dead there will come to life again and take their places in the bones of the building once more. I told Sophia something of this feeling once. She gave me a strange stare which at the time I put down to her mature, experienced outlook. Now I know she has no imagination and no soul. She could never understand the meaning of anything you can't touch or buy.

Being in the church comforted me. I wandered up to the lectern and ran my fingers over the huge, fierce, cool golden eagle perched on top. My fingers left a patterned, steamy mark on the bird's back. I gazed up at the stained glass and managed to make out the story of the Wedding at Cana. I sniffed the bowls of red roses and gypsophila. I gazed down at the polished brasses. Yes, I felt better.

And strangely, once out in that heat again, my feet took me not to my favourite spot on the side of the hill where I had first intended to go but to Mrs Gresham's house.

Perhaps it was the garden which drew me. It is always deliciously shady and secluded there. At the moment the apple trees are covered with little green bubbles of ripening apples and the lawn is a mass of daisies and clover. Mrs Gresham says it is not worth trying to preserve a lawn which has so many trees so she allows the daisies to grow freely. She has always said I may let myself into the garden any time even when she is not there. I suppose I half hoped she would be out, but she wasn't. She was sitting under a tree in a large white hat and a loose dress, reading. She looked wonderfully contented.

She glanced up and greeted me.

I stood quite still because suddenly I knew I was going to cry. I wanted to explain everything to her, and the fact that I was there, alone in the garden with her, made me feel very upset yet somehow released. She gazed at me for a moment and then laid down the book and asked if I would like a glass of lemonade.

She fetched it for me herself, and by the time she returned I had calmed down.

"I just thought I'd come and sit in the garden," I told her.

"That's fine. I'm glad you felt you could." She said no more, but took up her book again.

After I'd finished my drink I lay back on the grass. The leaves above dappled the sunlight. I gazed straight up at the blue sky through the apples and the leaves. It was too sad to lie there watching that glittering sky when I felt so dull, so I turned over and buried my nose in the grass. An ant tickled across my hand. It was very quiet.

I knew that if I wanted to talk I would have to speak first. Mrs Gresham would never try to make me talk. I heard her turn the pages.

Finally I said: "Sophia's mother has become one of those suffragettes. Are you surprised?"

She looked at me with her blue blue eyes. "No, Suzanna was always the one with spirit."

"How do you mean?" I asked.

"Well, as you know, we were quite a little group, your mother and Suzanna, Lady Middlecote and her sister, and me. Suzanna was the brilliant, pretty one. We all loved her, not just because she was so lovely, and children love beauty, but because of the things she said, and her energy. She was always so cheerful and eager for adventure."

She was silent for a while, gazing at me. "We all thought she would do something special. And then she met your uncle and I suppose she was dazzled by his money and his charm and the chances he offered her, and of course, being Suzanna, she quickly adapted herself to her new life. It's her way to be best at anything she does. But it is her way too, that if she should become aware that something is wrong, that her life is not as fine as she had imagined and hoped, that something is missing, she would rush out and look for something better. She tried a lover, and now she realises perhaps that it is her marriage and her gender that are trapping her, and so she seeks to alter that situation."

"Oh I should like to be free too!" I cried.

Mrs Gresham gave me an odd, questioning look. "Now what can you mean, Helen?"

"I feel trapped, Mrs Gresham. What hope is there for me?"

It was odd how I seemed to know what to say. This was not what I had intended to talk to her about when I first came to the garden. I had wanted to complain about Sophia.

"But I thought you loved Needlewick, Helen. Or has your cousin been giving you ambitions to go to London and become an ornament of society?"

"No," I replied loudly, "certainly not. All she wants is

to be like her mama used to be. I couldn't bear that existence. Anyway, I'm not beautiful enough."

She gave me a lovely smile. "No, my love, I daresay you're not."

"Oh, I used to admire Sophia but now I have realised that she has no real sympathy or imagination. I understand Aunt Suzanna better than Sophia does. I don't think Sophia can understand her mama at all."

I know Mrs Gresham is not fond of Sophia, and I had expected her to agree with me.

She stood up and came and sat beside me on the grass. "Helen, don't condemn Sophia, or stop loving her. You have given her so much, don't you see? You've shown her another side of life, perhaps a purer side, where people take pleasure from their family and friends and the countryside and are relatively content with these things, not always grasping after more money, more friends, more possessions."

"But I have stopped loving her. I can see straight through her. She does not care for anyone except herself."

At last Mrs Gresham said: "What has happened, Helen?"

"Nothing," I replied at once. But she sat still, waiting, in her billow of pale green skirt. "I showed her something very secret and precious and she laughed at it and destroyed it for me."

She was watching me closely. "Was it so important to you that one sneer from Sophia could cause it all to blow away? And don't you think, just possibly, that Sophia may have been cruel because she was envious? You have so much — a secure home, a loving family, and your independent spirit. You are a private person — Sophia is used to a surface world where no one dares look inside herself."

But I am not ready to forgive Sophia. "Anyway, I'll be glad when she's gone."

"Yes, I think so will I. You are not the same Helen any more." She softly tugged a lock of my hair and then returned to her book.

Soon afterwards I came home.

I know that the memory of this afternoon will remain firmly in my mind for a long time to come. I can smell the grass and the apples still, and hear the bees on the clover. I can remember the bird droppings on the wrought iron garden table, and the porch door of the house swung wide open, and I shan't forget any of it.

I have thought about what we said about Aunt Suzanna and about Sophia. And I have considered what Mrs Gresham said about my secret. A tiny grain of hope has come. Perhaps she is right. If I care enough, I shall be able to find my people again. And oddly, creeping after this hope, comes a sense of weariness. I do not think I have quite the energy to try and find them after all. It is such a long walk to the Tunnel Woods, and often when I go to see them they are not there and I waste my time.

Sophia has done this to me. She has drained me.

Sunday, 15 August

I do not know where I found the courage to do what I did last night.

Ever since Wednesday I seem to have heard Mrs Gresham's voice asking me over and over again whether my secret is really so important if it can be destroyed so easily. At first I didn't really want to try to find my people again at all, but yesterday morning I woke up feeling completely different. I could think of nothing but my people. I had to see them — I could not get the idea out of my mind. I'd be thinking of something different and then an image of the clearing would slip before my eyes.

But I couldn't visit them yesterday. First I had to go into Cheltenham with mother and Sophia, and when I returned I noticed that Michael was in the garden. How could I be sure he wouldn't follow me? So I waited.

Evening came and of course I thought I would not be able to go to them yesterday after all, it was too late. But then at supper the feeling that I must see them became so strong that I could scarcely eat.

I made the decision to visit them during the night.

I have always been a little frightened of the night. I gaze out of my window over the garden and the shrubs look so dark and hidden. How could I contemplate walking five miles mostly through woodlands on my own?

But I did. I couldn't stop myself.

My parents go to bed early, luckily. By ten-thirty the house was silent. I easily tiptoed out without waking anyone. And as I closed the garden door I remember thinking that I had closed the door on safety and warmth and I was out in the mysterious open air of the night. It smelt so good, slightly damp and very leafy, I could smell the night. I felt cheerful and strong as I plunged down the path towards the stream. There was a half moon. It was very starry. When I looked up I seemed to see more and more stars. They appeared to drop towards me out of the dark.

But as I neared the stream and entered the trees I felt less brave and excited. I almost turned back. I began to think that my people would not be there anyway in the night. And yet I'd been so sure. So sure. Each time I thought of turning back I'd think, "No, I'll go a little bit further, and then turn back." I tried not to imagine what may have lain behind the trees. I remembered my father's words when I once told him I was frightened of the night, "What could be hiding in the night, Helen, that is not there in the day?" I knew that this did not mean he would want me to be so far from home on my own, but the memory of those words comforted me.

Nevertheless, I was afraid. The night was so alive. There was a faint breeze which ruffled the leaves and sent the odd one scuffling down. The brook whispered and gurgled. I could hear more clearly than during the day. There were rustles in the leaves, birds or animals, I suppose, and the calls of night creatures. But the stream became a symbol of safety for me. While I was beside it, I told myself, nothing could happen to me.

Being in the woods was worse. The darkness plunged about me in fits and starts. I kept twisting my feet on roots or catching them in briars. The trees stooped above me, dark shapes. I tried to recognise them as the green-leafed, shining masses they are in the day but they seemed to be holding back from me. And as I stumbled up that steep path, I suddenly remembered the Tunnels. I had forgotten all about them. I wished I was back in my bed. I even wished Sophia was with me.

But I couldn't turn back. If I turned round, a host of terrible beings would be let loose from the Tunnels to follow me down the path. I must not turn my back on them.

I was half sobbing when I finally reached the square mouth of that first Tunnel. There was no light, none. I would be eaten up by blackness. But I had to go in because I had no choice. I could not turn my back on that blackness. I kept thinking: "It'll be two minutes, and then you'll be out in the bracken and nearer your people. Go to them, you'll be safe. They'll look after you." But all the time I knew that my people might not be there at all.

The dark was a physical barrier which I had to climb through. The blackness seemed to hit at my straining eyes and grope fingers through my hair. It had no mercy.

It breathed on my cheeks. My feet stepped into an abyss with each stride. I kept my hand on the wall and I never knew what I'd be touching next.

I was halfway along when I thought of bats. I imagined one landing on my face, wrapping its clammy wings about my eyes. I tightened my body, folded my arms, and half-closed my eyes, and all the time I imagined strange creatures were reaching out to me.

Until at last a dark grey light, as welcome as brilliant day to me, showed that I had come to the end, the gap between that first Tunnel and the next, and that I must climb up into the bracken.

But as I fumbled up the dark slope, something clutched at my left foot, half pulling off my boot. I tried to cry out but no sound came. I kicked and ran, reached the bracken and plunged into its dark, familiar fronds and hurtled forwards. Perhaps what had held me then was ivy or some other strong, climbing plant. Perhaps my foot was caught between two tightly packed rocks. I expect so.

I ran wildly, my throat hurting because my breath came in dry rasps. I ran. I ran. And stopped suddenly, amazed. For ahead of me, gleaming between the tall stems of bracken at either side of the path was light, soft, strong, orange light. I could smell my people, that composty odour of decaying leaves they always carry with them. I approached very slowly. And then suddenly I was no longer afraid, or anxious, or sad.

The light came from a huge fire which was lit in the centre of the clearing, near the hawthorn tree. It was near the tree, but not scorching it. The fire-light flung the tree into a new perspective. The branches stood out clearly, each leaf very separate, gleaming with orange light. There were no shadows within the tree, only light.

And they were there, around the fire, in the grass. And through them I could see the flames.

I sat by the fire in the heat of the flames, in the dancing, in the leaping flames which fingered the black night and the dancing and the music called me. The fire was hot and bright, the night beyond, the Tunnels were far away.

Come, leap.

I can leap through the flames, anything is possible. Leap. Leap.

But suddenly I knew I was leaping alone and I felt terribly afraid of being burnt.

You should never stop, never be afraid to leap alone.

But I was afraid. I couldn't do it any more.

I felt their hands on me. It was like being in a fever, feeling first burning hot and then cool and damp. Their hands soothed the scalding wounds. I felt them stroking and caressing. And as they touched me, they began to ease me away from the fire. I should have held back. I wish now I'd held back. But I didn't. It was so beautiful to be gently and soothingly brought away. . . . away. Everything seemed to be fading around me, as if I was fainting and the darkness was rushing through me.

After a while it came to me that I was alone on the edge of the woods. I turned. The woods were dark behind me. I felt cold as I looked at them. The top of the valley was bright by contrast. I was on the path they had shown me, the quick way home. I walked out into the open fields feeling free and strong and beautiful. I was out in the soft night with the stars falling around me, the breeze ruffling my hair and the fields away to my left. It was good to be part of the night.

I hesitated a while at the garden gate, but the smell of the flowers within the garden lured me finally, although I knew that, once inside, the night would be gone from me and the magic would drift away.

The roses and mignonette seemed heavier with scent than during the day. They were quite still, like china flowers, for the high garden wall sheltered them from the breeze outside.

I touched them. When I was little I used to kiss the trunks of trees because I loved them, they seemed to me so kindly and firm. I loved their rough bark against my lips. Last night I would have done the same, but once in the garden I felt eyes in the night and I was afraid to stay long or do anything strange. I had returned to the old world of doubts and fears.

The house felt stiflingly warm but the sheets and soft mattress of my bed were wonderful. I was exhausted.

Wednesday, 18 August

It is Sophia's fault that I lied to her. I couldn't help myself. It was she who taught me to lie. She has been lying since her arrival — about what she really thinks of us all and about how much she cares for me. She made me want to lie to pay her back. And I wanted to defeat her, to send her home beaten, even if she never realises it.

She has laughed at everything about my life here, I feel that now. She believes her own family, her own way of life to be so right, to be so much better than anything anyone else could ever be. She's so untouchable in her superiority that I wanted to withhold just one thing from her, to keep one thing out of her reach. And she'll never know what it is. I'm loving this lie because she'll never know about it.

The other reason is her stupid camera. Ever since her brother sent it she's been showing it off. She can use it, I can't. She keeps offering to let me have a go but I won't. I won't touch anything of hers. I won't owe her anything. So we've been all round the village with her Kodak because she must have something to remind her of lovely

Needlewick. And of course, I knew it was coming, she must photograph the clearing, it's become such a special place to her she says, because of me. And she will send me a print, wouldn't I love that — to have a print of the clearing? And of course photographs can be very revealing, she says.

So on Monday we went back to the Tunnel Woods.

Oh, she thought she was very grand, swinging her little Kodak on its strap, talking about the advantages of hand-held cameras and how expert her brother is at photography. And all the time I knew the clearing would be a dead place. Since Saturday night I have known that my people have really gone for ever from me. Their last gift for me was their dance. I did expect there would be the charred remains of the fire and foolishly mentioned it to Sophia, wanting to show off, I suppose. I had intended to pick up some ashes as a last souvenir. But there was nothing. The clearing was absolutely bare.

I let her take some photographs of course. Why not? She might as well waste her precious film.

But on the way home I realised that this revenge was not enough. I wanted to hurt her and frighten her in the way I had been frightened.

She spent yesterday in Needlewick, playing the rich, charming heiress, distributing toffees to the Makepeace children and making them stand in a bunch outside their cottage while she took their picture. She didn't include Mrs Makepeace. I suppose she thought the children looked sweet, whereas their mother might have added a touch of real sadness to the scene.

Sophia then sailed up the High Street, took a photograph of the church, and arrived at the Greshams' house. To my surprise Mrs Gresham didn't seem to mind posing for her. In the picture she will be standing beneath her favourite tree, clasping her hat, her skirts sailing out behind her in the breeze. Sophia also took a picture of

Roundstones and the servants and my parents in the garden. My father stood with one hand on Michael's shoulder. Neither Michael nor Mrs Bubb were smiling; Mrs Bubb gazed straight ahead at the camera, Michael looked away down to the river. I hated Sophia for taking this photograph. She will be carrying part of my home back with her, stealing something away.

We are having a party in her honour tomorrow night, and then, at last, she will be gone.

I got my revenge. But I do not feel happy tonight as I thought I would, only disturbed and somehow dirtied because it all worked so well, she was so frightened.

We went again to the clearing.

We were very much at odds. She kept trying to win me over. She said frequently how much she'd miss me and how noisy London would seem compared to Needlewick. Then she tried to gain my pity by saying that she feared seeing her mother again after all that had happened. But I said as little as possible and was very sulky. And because I hated being like that and kept remembering what Mrs Gresham had said about trying to love Sophia, several times I was near the point of taking her arm and making a sign of forgiveness. But I couldn't. And I had to go on with my stupid plan. I had this feeling that I must do it, I couldn't stop myself. My will was pushing me on and I couldn't prevent it from happening.

When we came near to the Tunnels on the way home I suggested we should try a game I used to play during recreation at school. It is called "Trust". One person is blindfolded, the other has to direct her to do whatever she wants. If you trust the other person you will do what she says. Sophia clearly thought I was being very childish but she consented because she was determined to be kind to me. I believe she quite enjoyed the game at first. I blindfolded her and led her about and called directions to her. Then we reversed positions. I stood in the dark while she told me to take three steps, turn to the left, walk backwards two steps and so on. She was good at that; she likes being obeyed. I felt the bracken around me and was very excited because of what I was going to do next.

When I had blindfolded her again I took her hand and led her down into the gap between the two Tunnels. She squeaked with fear as we climbed down the stony slope. Once at the bottom, I twisted her round and round and then led her not into our usual Tunnel but to the other, far longer Tunnel which she had never been in before. Then I tiptoed away. At first she called after me, laughing, but I didn't reply. Then she grew a little annoyed and announced that she would remove the blindfold. But I had tied an intricate, very tight knot, and wound the scarf's fringe into her hair so it took her a while to drag the blindfold off. Then she began to walk down the Tunnel in the direction I had hoped, the wrong direction, away from the gap in the Tunnels and the way home. I followed her very quietly in the dark. Once or twice I think she heard me because she stopped dead and called my name rather nervously.

At last she reached the exit and began to walk along the path. She did not seem to realise for a while that the path was unfamiliar to her.

Then, when it began to slope upwards instead of down, she shouted, "Helen, Helen where are you? Don't play the fool. Please! Come on!" But I remained hidden. I believe she was almost in tears by this time, but I had my best trick to come, and I wasn't going to give myself away. She turned round and began to walk very fast back in the direction of the Tunnels. I was ready for her.

I had remained hidden near the entrance. I raced back along the Tunnel and scrambled up the rubble slope which leads to the path to the clearing. But instead of going that way, I branched off over the top of the second Tunnel until I came to the opening of the air vent I discovered last summer. My hands were full of pebbles. When I heard Sophia's hurrying footsteps below I let drop a shower of pebbles. She screamed and stopped dead. I continued to drop one pebble at a time. I'd allow a long pause, then, when I heard her take a step, I'd drop another. Each pebble clattered softly down the vent, making an echo of itself.

I could hear her sobbing.

Eventually I ran out of pebbles. It must have been ten minutes before a rustle made me realise she was creeping along the wall of the Tunnel. Seconds later she was out into the daylight, racing down the path. I followed more slowly and eventually ran to catch up with her beside the stream.

"Where did you get to?" I cried.

She gave a start and turned to me. Her hair was untidy, her face pale and swollen with crying and her beautiful flower-print dress stained where she had rubbed it along the side of the Tunnel.

"That was cruel," she whispered.

"What was?" I exclaimed. I felt frightened. "I turned round and you had gone. You must have wandered off up the wrong Tunnel."

She looked at me with baffled eyes for a moment and then said: "Oh Helen, thank heavens you're here. I was so afraid."

I allowed her to link her hand in my arm, although I hated her even more now I had got my revenge on her.

I feel sad and dirty tonight. She deserved to be made unhappy but I didn't know I could be so cruel. I keep thinking of the Helen who was writing only a month ago how much she loved her cousin, and of the excited, tight feeling at the top of my legs as I dropped the pebbles.

Wednesday, 25 August

Sophia has written a long, moaning, selfish letter full of lies about how she longs to be back here again. She is having to face some difficulties in London so I suppose she feels it would be far easier for her if she were back in Needlewick.

Good. Good. I'm glad her family has broken up. I'm glad her mother has gone away.

My mother is very upset by the news and cannot understand why Aunt Suzanna has left, but I can. I can. My uncle sounds a hateful man. Looking back through this diary I see that I once admired the life Sophia's mother used to lead. How wrong I was! How childish to be taken in by the fact that Aunt Suzanna wore gorgeous clothes and went to parties. Her life must then have been as empty and futile as Sophia's will be.

Mrs Gresham has been talking to mother, trying to make her understand about Aunt Suzanna but of course mother will never understand. She is so happy at home doing exactly what she likes best, endless little domestic chores and calls. How could she understand her sister's new, violent way of life?

I cannot bring myself to reply to Sophia. I have nothing to say to her now. I cannot tell her what I really think — it would be a waste because she certainly wouldn't understand. I cannot write affectionately to her, that would be a lie and I have lied enough. And if I write she will reply and I do not want to hear from her again. Her letter makes me unhappy because it is from her and I want to forget her.

What a child I was before she came! I was so happy here, wandering about, friendly with all the village, content to let my schooldays drift by. I had the clearing and that was enough for me.

The clearing, ah yes, what a mystery all that is.

Already it is all gently fading from my memory. I would not dream of going back to the Tunnel Woods, because I know I'll never see my people again. But I don't feel sad, no, almost glad to be free of that secret, to be free of knowing them and having to visit them. And that is odd because in the years I knew them I never thought of them as being a burden to me, not once. They were my dearest friends. But now I feel as if they never gave me very much after all. Oh, they were a precious secret, intriguing and amusing, but they taught me little really. They only made me happy.

Happy! I wonder how long it will be before I feel happy again. I feel utterly discontented.

I walk round and round the garden, kicking at plants, blaming Sophia for ruining everything with her boredom, her unhappy family, her scorn for all the things I used to love about my home. Now I see through her eyes what a tiny world we live in here. Nothing happens. Some people live in Needlewick all their lives, never once venturing even to Cheltenham. They have no desire to see the world beyond.

But I certainly have now. I feel as if I have not stretched my limbs properly for years. I must extend my mind and thoughts. I must get away and learn what is going on. I always used to think Needlewick would be enough for me. I'd marry some local man and live the same life that my mother has always lived, quiet, sheltered and untroubled. But now other places are calling to me. Needlewick is only the beginning.

Mrs Gresham thinks I could make a career for myself if I set my mind to it. How grand that word career sounds! I have decided that my way of escape is to choose a career which will require that I should go away. My father went to Cambridge and then to a hospital in London. I don't think I shall be a doctor, but I should like to study in a university. Mrs Gresham says there are scholarships to be won.

I shall tell no one of this. My mother would be amazed if she knew of my plans, and my father would think it was an amusing girlish whim. So I'll keep quiet. I shall just go ahead and do it on my own.

I have learnt to keep my secrets close.

8

BY THE TIME she laid aside the diary Sophia was cramped and chilled and the light was fading. The willow cast a long black shadow over her. Her face and neck were wet with tears.

She stood, went to the river and gazed along its bank in the direction of the Tunnel Woods. She had forgotten so much. The river flowed in dark ripples — she had to restrain her hand from releasing the notebooks to the water. The river could not carry away all her guilt. She had arranged such a cosy, nostalgic afternoon for herself; she had planned to sit by the willow and indulge in a package of memories, expecting to smile fondly at her childish follies and then at last to leave behind the Needlewick ghosts which had quietly pursued her down the years. Instead she was weeping with fear of the ghosts crowding insistently about her. She loved you, they said, and you destroyed her love. She gave you all she had, and you pushed it away. Your mother was there, calling for help, but you ignored her. Nicholas, clear-sighted, kind, was treated through your letters to a showy parade of arrogant drivel.

Mrs Gresham, how could you be so cruel as to confront me with all this?

She became conscious of the night — of small noises in the reeds and grasses. She yearned for warmth, company and light. If only Colin were here, she thought, he'd look after me and comfort me. But Colin was far away, she had not wanted him to come to Needlewick.

Her feet were wet with dew by the time she reached the house. She let herself in by the kitchen door, hoping not to attract attention, but Mrs Bubb was standing there, as if waiting for her.

"I've kept your supper warm," was all she said, unsmiling as ever, but for the first time Sophia detected a little warmth in the slightly bulbous grey eyes, as well as a definite craving.

Sophia crept up to her room, washed her face and descended to the drawing-room.

Her aunt leapt to her feet. "Sophia! Where have you been, dear? You've missed supper. Of course it doesn't matter, we've kept you some. Oh, you look so pale!" She kindly did not draw attention to Sophia's eyes which were red and dazzled.

"I went for a walk, further than I intended."

"Oh, you should have waited for me. It's so lonely on your own. I was saying so to Jane this afternoon."

The doctor, in a rare display of consideration, interrupted with an offer of brandy.

"Yes, yes, a small glass of brandy would be very welcome. And if you don't mind I'll take it up to my room. I feel so tired."

"Of course, of course, and I'll bring you up your supper," her aunt suggested. "We must look after you, you must eat or what will your father think of us? Would you like some hot milk too?"

"No, really, thank you, aunt, and I'll collect my supper from the kitchen. Really, don't worry." Sophia stooped to kiss her. "Good night. Thank you."

Her aunt was easy to please. All she asked was a little affection. Sophia hated herself for buying a little glow of happiness so cheaply, with one kiss.

9

MRS PARDITER DID not approve of Needlewick's new vicar; he was young, unmarried, apparently radical theologically and, according to his housekeeper, drank rather heavily. She therefore felt no compunction at not listening to his sermon on the Beatitudes and elected instead to concentrate her attention on his flock. The Middlecote pew, set at right angles and elevated from the rest, commanded a good view of the nave. In particular she could see the Callwoods: Harry, with the dreamy expression that signified a mental sleep; Margaret, her countenance shut up and worried; and Sophia, face shadowed by an absurdly heavy hat brim, eyes fixed on prayer book, lips compressed. But, despite the inadequacy of her view of Sophia's expression, Deborah Parditer could detect that a light had gone out in her, the confidence and youthful consciousness that had brought such vitality to the drawing-room at Roundstones had drained away.

She's seen the diary then, Deborah realised, and it has moved her, as of course it should. Deborah had read it herself during one of her vigils by Eleanor Gresham's bedside in the last weeks of her life.

Eleanor had usually said little, being content to lie and listen to chapters from a favourite book, but one night she had told Deborah in her clear, deliberate voice: "I shall leave Helen's diary to Sophia."

"Which diary, Eleanor?"

"Oh, didn't you know? Helen used to keep a diary. She came to me once, years ago now, and told me that she was going to destroy it because she'd outgrown it. She made this announcement so solemnly. And I — well — even all those years ago I'm afraid I used a sick woman's privilege. I asked her if she'd let me have it."

"And she didn't mind?"

"Not at all. I think, if anything, she was rather flattered. But she would not look at the diary again herself. She made me promise to throw it away after I'd read it."

"Sensible girl."

"Yes, perhaps. And perhaps I should not have asked."

"It was an odd request!"

"Yes. I know. But Helen was already far different from the dreamy little girl she once was. I thought her diary would remind me of her. It did, but only in that same pointlessly sad way that photographs reveal how time has passed and things have changed. So I only read it once. But there was one part I couldn't burn. It contained too much of Suzanna."

After a little pause during which Deborah dwelt on the meaning of this remark, she asked: "Has John written to Suzanna about you, yet?"

"No. I won't let him write."

"She should know about your condition."

"She will know. But I won't have her come home out of pity for me."

"Eleanor!"

At last Eleanor admitted sadly: "It does seem a long time since I heard from her."

Deborah was seated in a low chair by the drawn

curtains; in the lamplight she could see that her friend had turned her head away. The intimacy of the room had become suddenly oppressive. Mention of Suzanna always seemed to have a jarring effect, there were too many conflicting thoughts, too much unsaid, too many shared and unshared memories.

But suddenly Eleanor murmured softly: "You may read the diary if you like, Deborah. I'm sure Helen wouldn't mind. Read it."

Deborah felt an instant of childish suspicion — how many times had Suzanna, or Eleanor, or both, flung a book or letter at her: "Oh, let her read it. Go on, she's dying to read it! Go on then, Deborah!" Was Eleanor mocking her now, humouring her curiosity? But no, this was being offered as a gift; Eleanor's eyes were full of warmth, even laughter. "I'd like you to read it," she added softly. "I'm very tired now. It's there on the chest-of-drawers, do you see?"

When the congregation rose for the offertory, Sophia's pale face was lifted to the pulpit for an instant. And now that poor girl has read it too, thought Deborah. I hope she is brash enough not to take it much to heart. It happened so long ago, and none of it was her fault really. Indeed, did not I, when faced with the same imponderable obsession, react the same way? Or would have done, had I been allowed a little closer? But Suzanna shut me out. She was much wiser than Helen, and chose her confidante well.

The pain, even after all those years, was still very sharp, sharper far than that of bereavement for her husband or even for Eleanor. The pain of exclusion.

Arriving at Roundstones on a spring morning to find Mrs Bubb in the kitchen, her knuckles rubbed red and raw with the toil of washday, her face shuttered, but a triumphant flicker in her eye. "The girls have gone out long since. They've left me all this lot."

"Did they say where they were going, Mrs Bubb?"

"Not a word, no."

But she knew.

Up went Deborah's chin. "Come on, Jane, we'll go and call on Eleanor. Come on. We'll go riding."

Riding, riding, the great salve; the Henshaw girls' way of excluding the others, for only they were privileged enough as daughters of a wealthy farmer to be good horsewomen.

But just by chance they would be down by the river at the end of the day to see Suzanna and Margaret come trailing home: Suzanna first, swinging her hat, her eyes aglow, her step buoyant; Margaret behind, tight-lipped and exhausted.

"Hello Deborah, hello Jane! Oh, my dears, we've had such a day!"

Suzanna was always so full of love at the end of those trips that it oozed out of her and fell on them, spilling and softening until they melted in her warmth and forgave her. But there were never apologies, nor explanations either from radiant Suzanna or loyal Margaret. And the Henshaw girls and Eleanor Carney could not understand what had won their friend away.

"What does she do there?" they would whisper in the shelter of the willow. "Why does she keep going to the Tunnel Woods?"

"Mrs Bubb knows," perceptive Eleanor remarked. "But then she would."

"Why would she?"

"She watches us all. Didn't you know? Anyway, she's been here so long."

"Shall we ask her?"

"Don't be silly! As if she'd tell us."

"But what do you think she does there, Eleanor? You must have an idea. Doesn't Margaret say?"

But Eleanor was suffering too much from Suzanna's complete defection. "I don't know, and I certainly can't be bothered to find out. If she wants to spend her life traipsing up and down that wretched Tunnel, let her. And poor Margaret has to drag after her! She should be more thoughtful."

"Perhaps she's got a lover there," ventured Jane daringly.

"She wouldn't hide that!" Eleanor retorted dismissively and went to throw pebbles into the river, first a handful in an angry splatter, then one at a time as she listened for the delicate plop. "Anyway," she called, "you can be sure it won't last. You can be sure of that! She'll move on to something else before too long. Suzanna can stick at nothing."

But in this she was wrong. It was so long before Suzanna was released from her passion that the Henshaw girls had put up their hair and become absorbed in a social round of picnics and evening parties; and Eleanor Carney had begun to study in earnest, dreaming and scheming to get away from Needlewick to a university. Meanwhile poor Margaret had worn through many a pair of shoes in pursuit of her wayward sister's light footsteps along the path to the Tunnel Woods. And then it was only because, one day, emerging from the woods by an upper path, they had met a man on horseback, and Simon Theobald's eyes had fallen on the clear transfigured face of Suzanna, that the spell was broken.

Looking now at the daughter of that union, kneeling in prayer where for eighteen years her mother had knelt each Sunday, Deborah thought: There can be no question of an easy life for you, my lamb, if there's anything at all of your mother in you. But yes, I think one day you will thank Eleanor Gresham for bringing you back here and showing you these things. There are cards other than those your father would deal you. And your mother has played a fistful and lost the lot, but is that, after all, the worst possible fate?

10

SOPHIA TOOK THE path to the Tunnel Woods.
The air was moist and heavy but promised warmth later and the river was so still that the rustle of a bird in the undergrowth was startling. She had brought the diary.

Walking was a struggle. Such was her sense of misery and dismay that the pain in her heart seemed to thrust out to her stomach, knees and shoulders. It was the extent of her self-delusion that hurt so much; the memory of her feeling of triumph at that wretched wedding, for instance, the consciousness then of her own superior polish and beauty beside her dowdy country cousin. Reading the diary had made the events of that summer return with such clarity: the hot sunny days she had grown to savour once her homesickness had diminished; the long dragging expeditions along this same path with Helen; the terrible afternoon when she had been lost in the Tunnels. The photographs she had taken then were tucked away in her writing box at home, faded, uninteresting prints she had salvaged from Nicholas's desk after his death. And all that summer of 1909 she had felt so gloriously good for Helen, such a breath of air, such company, as she filled her cousin's head with new ideas and opened the world for her.

She had of course wondered at Helen's cruelty on that last day at the Tunnels — indeed there was much about Helen she had wondered at, but then dismissed. Helen after all was such a simple soul, living in a fantasy world with which Sophia had ostensibly sympathised but inwardly treated with incredulity and derision. It was only when Helen failed to reply to her subsequent letters from London that Sophia had become mystified and upset. She had written so revealingly about the situation at home: her mother's desertion, her father's self-absorption and Nicholas suddenly so grown-up he was out of reach. From Helen she had expected sympathy and understanding but received nothing. Now Sophia could recognise her cousin's last, belated attempt at self-preservation; now Helen's final hatred for her burned through the shabby covers of the diary.

It was undeserved, Sophia argued inwardly, she thought I planned that stupid trick with Michael — she might have known I would have had nothing to do with him. But Sophia's conscience rebuked her with the knowledge that her actual betrayal had been more constant and more cruel and had begun the instant she set foot from the train with her shiny hair, smart hat and condescending airs. From the first she had despised Helen for her lack of affectation, her kindness and her determination to love and admire this exotic creature from London.

And, as Sophia now acknowledged, she had found Helen's strangeness particularly irritating. Helen had always ultimately eluded her, for she could retreat to a place where no one could follow. And the diary made clear that she really had believed in those people of hers. She had become completely enchanted by her own fantasies. Sophia now realised that she had underestimated the potency of her cousin's imagination. But surely, she thought in self-justification, no-one could have understood her — surely any sane person would have acted as I did, and laughed at her?

Yet the hem of her frock was now wet because she was hurrying along the path to the Tunnel Woods, drawn by curiosity and a sense that her pilgrimage to Needlewick would somehow be incomplete unless she returned there. She needed to be vindicated by the ordinariness of the clearing.

She had forgotten how far it was. Nothing seemed familiar, though she passed through coppices and fields which must have been unchanged for generations. She became convinced that she would never reach the Tunnel Woods though she knew that they at least were real. The path was overgrown, but it was still used and she wondered who would wish to walk there. Increasingly she felt ill-at-ease, even to the point of wishing Colin had been with her; she would have welcomed his companionship, even while perversely resenting the intrusion. Not that she would have allowed him to read the diary, of course.

Perhaps Mr Gresham would have come. He would understand her curiosity. And this thought brought her back to the same nagging questions. Why, why had Helen given the diary to Mrs Gresham? And why had it in turn been bequeathed to Sophia? The knowledge that Mrs Gresham's delicate hands had turned the pages gave Sophia cause to shudder. What must she have thought of the cousins' behaviour? Yet Sophia's heart had contracted as she read of the conversation in the garden at The Grey House as reported by Helen. Far from dismissing Sophia, Mrs Gresham had seen and pitied her weakness. And what had been her view of Helen's experiences in the clearing?

Sophia was soon tired. Though the sun had not yet

broken through the mist, it was already very warm. Then, quite suddenly, she saw that she was nearly at the woods. The trees which had intermittently edged the path grew closer together; ahead the river twisted away amidst dense woodland. But her way was barred by a high fence. The path had been deliberately blocked — and not recently judging by the weathering of the tall stakes and the height of the vegetation which had grown up against them. Sophia stood several feet away, as if measuring herself against the obstacle. She did not have the nerve to pit her untried female body in its light linen dress against the awkwardness of the fence. She simply could not imagine herself attempting to cross over. She looked wearily along its length. As far as she could remember the woods had always been private property and always fenced. This new addition simply closed up their narrow access.

But why is the path so well-used, she thought indignantly? What is the point of anyone coming along here at all?

The fruitlessness of her expedition and a sense of her own weakness brought tears of frustration as she plodded angrily away. What does it matter, anyway? she pondered. It is unlike me to bother much about anything. Nothing has affected me deeply since Nicholas's death. So what does this matter? I have read the diary and it has made me uncomfortable for a while. Well, let this be an end to it.

But she thought again of Mrs Gresham, who had been dying faster than most, even as she freewheeled her bicycle down the hill or supplied visitors with tea and cake in her sunlit garden. Sophia had disliked her for seeing through her careful veneer to the conceited, uncertain child beneath. But for some reason she had thought enough about Sophia to give her the diary. Why, Mrs Gresham?

Someone was fishing from the river bank, his back bent as if he'd nodded asleep, yet as Sophia approached she saw that his head was raised, his eyes fixed intently on the river. She was not too disturbed to see him there, for she was nearing Roundstones and had anyway been half expecting him. However, she determined to gain the initiative at once.

"Caught anything?" she called.

He did not move his head, merely responded: "I could have told you they'd blocked the path."

She had intended to walk purposefully on, but now checked her pace. "How did you know I'd go there?"

"Of course you would. Where else would you go?"

"Why are the stakes there?"

"They've been there for years now. Soon after you were here last. It's private land. They can do what they like with it."

She suddenly became aware of his eyes on the diary in her hand. He showed no curiosity, only a kind of satisfaction. She hid the notebooks in the fold of her skirt.

"I know a way in," he said.

"Do you?"

"I'll take you sometime if you like."

"Oh, it's kind of you but I don't think I'll bother again. I only wanted a little walk, for old time's sake."

He shrugged. "Let me know when you change your mind."

"Thank you."

As she walked away she was aware of his gaze on her back. Even after she had rounded a bend in the river she did not feel unwatched.

*

Entering the garden at Roundstones by the door in the wall she found herself facing a little gathering on the lawn and, at its centre, quite at home with three middle-aged ladies and an elderly country practitioner, Colin.

Retreat was impossible for they'd all seen her. She adopted a surprised, delighted smile, suitable for an unlooked for appearance of the betrothed, and held out her hands to him.

"Colin, what a marvellous surprise!"

"I thought I'd come. I'd heard so much about this village and I wanted to save you the train journey home."

She could tell that he was a little apprehensive about what her reaction might be, but she behaved impeccably. "My dear, I'm delighted to see you. But poor Aunt Margaret, what a shock for her! You should have let us know. We do have a telephone."

"Oh Sophia, I don't mind at all. Not at all. And he's not staying here, he says, though of course we'd gladly put him up, I suppose he could have had Helen's room without. . . . But he's got friends in Cheltenham, he says, well of course you'd know. But we are all so pleased to be able to meet him." Aunt Margaret's anxious, gratified smile took in her two friends from Middlecote Hall who were undoubtedly impressed by this grand visitor.

"You should have told me you were coming," Sophia remarked again teasingly. "I could have been gone hours yet! I've been rediscovering my childish haunts."

"I've been hearing all about you from your aunt and Lady Middlecote here — what an impression you made on Needlewick last time you came. Sophia can't avoid making an impact on people," he added fondly.

"If you want tea, Sophia," said her uncle, "you'll have to go and get it. This has gone cold."

She retreated thankfully to the kitchen, though there

she was subjected to the scrutiny of Mrs Bubb's inquisitive gaze. The housekeeper was drinking tea at the kitchen table. Sophia reflected, with some surprise, that this was the first time she had seen her sit down.

"He's come for you then," Mrs Bubb stated.

"You mean Lord Kilbride?" Sophia responded coolly, replenishing the teapot from the kettle. "Yes, he's very kindly offered to drive me home."

"I like him."

"I'm pleased to hear it."

"I never liked your father."

Sophia was so surprised by this unwarranted confidence that her response was unguarded. "I didn't know you'd ever met my father properly."

"Oh yes, he came here often when he was courting her. I knew he wasn't right."

"No."

"He didn't like Needlewick, of course. He wanted her away."

"I think she was ready to leave, don't you Mrs Bubb? I don't think my mother would have been very happy if she'd stayed here all her life."

"Happy! What's happiness?" The words were spoken with contempt.

Sophia took Colin down to the footbridge where they leaned on the rail and gazed down into the clear water, watching the slim reeds bend in the current.

"Helen used to drop sticks in here. She wanted me to play a racing game with her, but I never would. I always tried to be so grown-up," Sophia said.

"You sound sad."

"Do I? I'm not sad, of course I'm not. You're here. I'm very flattered you should come all this way for me."

"I missed you," he said suddenly. "You don't know. God, God I've missed you."

She stood upright and pressed the base of her spine against the rail. "Don't be silly! You must be far too busy to miss me!"

But he took her fingers and kissed them softly and laying his hands on her waist began to kiss her cheeks, lips and chin. She obediently held his shoulders and daringly responded by opening her lips and teeth, but drew back in alarm after a while, oppressed and a little bored. She averted her face and gave him a shy smile.

"We'll be seen."

"I don't care. I love you. I don't care who knows."

She was used to him telling her he loved her, but for once the implications of the words came home to her and she felt bowed down by the weight of responsibility they gave her. She laid her finger on his cheek. "My love."

11

THE VERDICT AT Middlecote Hall later was that Colin was "a nice boy, such a nice boy, didn't you think, Jane?".

"Yes, I thought so."

They were at dinner in the cold dining-room where the food lay in over-large dishes on the white table cloth, waiting for Sir George to snort and wheeze his way through a second helping.

"Of course you won't have met him, George," persisted Deborah, who always tried to draw him into conversations out of a sense of duty and an even stronger feeling of irritation that anyone could be so incapable of taking an interest in anything other than his own worthless pursuits (claret, cigars, food, guns, horses, felons). "There's not a trace of the Scot in him — I must ask Sophia about the Kilbride name."

"Oh you wouldn't expect him to have an accent, surely?" asked Jane.

"Not an accent, but one can usually tell. I can always tell."

"Did you expect him to be wearing a kilt?"

Deborah's attention was momentarily caught by the

size of the load on her brother-in-law's fork.

"Delightful, old-fashioned manners," she murmured. "You could see he was a gentleman."

But later, when the sisters were snugly installed in the sitting-room and Sir George safely splayed out in his chair, his head flung back on the carefully preserved antimacassar, a half-smoked cigar in the ash-tray, Deborah said: "Of course he's not at all right for Sophia."

"Deborah!"

"He's much too straightforward, don't you think? And she doesn't love him."

"You have no right to say that, Deborah. You shouldn't make such pronouncements. I couldn't help thinking how well suited they seemed. He's so fond of her, and she does need some one like him, the poor child, she's had no-one but the father all these years."

"That may be so, but I'm right. He's no use to her, not unless there's more to him than meets the eye."

"He's a very successful barrister, you know. He's no fool."

"He may be clever, but that's not quite what I meant."

"You talk about Sophia as if she's completely uncontrollable. All the poor girl needs is a little care. She'll soon lose that slightly hard edge she has."

"So you've noticed it? Even you. She's not uncontrollable, no. She doesn't need controlling, what an ugly word. Good Lord, Jane, she's a modern woman! But how will he deal with Suzanna, for instance?"

"Deal with her?"

"Of course, sooner or later she'll appear. And then what? How will Lord Kilbride feel then, in the midst of some dreadful Theobald reunion? She may even come to the wedding."

"He looks perfectly capable of dealing with any such eventuality."

"Oh he'll be charming to Suzanna, as he is to everyone. But he won't take her on."

"Why should he take her on? He's not marrying her."

"Oh Good Lord, Jane! Sometimes I think you try to be stupid to irritate me."

It's not that I'm stupid, Jane thought later, it's simply that I don't find it easy to judge, or at least I don't trust my conclusions as Deborah does.

And indeed, she had certainly learnt not to presume anything about Suzanna.

When Simon Theobald's presence in Suzanna's life had become known to the Henshaw girls, Jane had been bowled over by the romance of it. A wealthy Londoner, looking at some land with a view to purchase, had literally come across Suzanna and Margaret in the soft orange twilight of a May evening and sat above them astride his horse, his eyes never leaving Suzanna's face while Margaret, to whom he had addressed an enquiry, told him the way to Needlewick.

Of course the Henshaw girls had no cause to meet him for several weeks for they were by then far too old to spy from the footbridge or gossip in the sweetshop, on the lookout for Suzanna. Indeed, Deborah was preoccupied with her own marriage at that time, surrounded by lists and trunks and sewing, in her element at last, with little time to listen to Jane's breathless accounts of this most wonderful Needlewick love-affair.

But Jane had pondered on it far into the nights, lying on her back in bed as she imagined Suzanna with the evening sun on her face as she raised her eyes to meet those of the stranger from London. Jane was kept informed of the progress of the courtship by Eleanor who called occasionally for tea and to help with Deborah's sewing. And at last Jane was to meet him at Deborah's wedding, not of course at the ceremony for he was too new a feature of Suzanna's life to be invited to that, but at the evening party.

He was a striking figure, very tall beside slender Suzanna, but his handshake was firm and warm. Jane was intimidated by his good looks, particularly by the unusual blue of his eyes and the clear bone structure of nose and chin. And Suzanna was as if shot about with static electricity, her smile brilliant and the contours of her face somehow finer; her hair bright beneath a little posy of white roses, one of which, Jane noticed distinctly, still had a drop of dew on its outer petal. And Jane, who had been left untouched by the nuptials that same morning of her sister and Gerald Parditer, knew that Simon Theobald's hand had placed those flowers in Suzanna's hair, and could sense that his flesh had brushed her friend's ear and cheek.

Of course Simon had no interest in plain Jane Henshaw — although Suzanna introduced her as "one of my best friends" — and Jane's tongue turned to damp sand at the prospect of talking to him. But later, after the third of her now customary series of dances with George Middlecote, she had tiptoed out into the garden and seen them kissing under the vine on the verandah. Simon's hands were cupped under Suzanna's chin; they stood for several moments quite still and then he dipped his head and kissed her. After a while his hands dropped from her face and his arms encircled her so that she was a little pinioned doll in his grasp. The force of the kiss; the fusion of their two mouths was never forgotten by Jane, who crept away and quietly unmanned poor Sir George by appearing at his side and gently taking his hand.

But sexual energy, it would appear, wasn't enough. My marriage, thought Jane, lying beneath her white and pink hand-stitched quilt in the bedroom she had long ceased to share with George, has lasted, and Suzanna's didn't.

12

COLIN DROVE SOPHIA home to London on Monday morning. She was not ready to leave but could find no excuse for staying. She sat beside him in a tense rage. He had cut short her visit to Needlewick. She had certainly missed his company at times, but not enough to outweigh her distress at his intrusion. She was still raw from her first reading of the diary and had wanted to spend more time at Roundstones in the hope of finding a balm there. She had decided to discover a way into the Tunnel Woods, to prove there was nothing there — or as an apology to Helen. And she'd had no time to say a proper goodbye to kind Lady Middlecote or her sister, who would doubtless consider this sudden departure disrespectful. Worst of all, she'd seen no more of Mr Gresham. He might think her childish or indifferent, rushing away like this.

Although she explained nothing to Colin, he could not be oblivious to her rigid posture, averted shoulder or silken, monosyllabic replies.

Finally he stopped the car where the lane widened by a farm track, took her hand and asked why she was upset.

She had been so obsessed by her anger that she could not for a moment see how he could fail to understand her.

"Is it anything to do with me?" he added.

His nose was very pink from the rush of air on his face; he looked too boyish and foolish to warrant being hurt.

"Nothing's wrong," she replied. "I simply didn't want to leave Needlewick."

"Oh, I thought you would have had more than enough of it by now. It's such a tiny place. Your father thought I'd be doing you a favour by rescuing you."

"Was it on his suggestion, then, that you came?"

"Partly, but it didn't take much persuasion." He picked up her gloved hand and kissed it.

Sophia softened a little. "I remember last time I didn't want to come home either. But that wasn't because of Needlewick, it was because I was terrified of what I might find at home."

"What did you find?"

"Oh God, it's so sordid. You must know the whole story. Nicholas had warned me by letter, but it was far worse than I expected. Mother was gone, just gone. Father was in a brutal, silent state. Nicholas retreated into his studies. My father wouldn't even let us speak about mother, or my time in Needlewick. I somehow came to think that the two events — my being away in Needlewick and her leaving home — were connected."

"They possibly were."

"I don't think so. No, of course not. My mother would have gone off whether I'd been there or not. She'd had enough of her life at home and wanted to branch out a bit. My father, by the way, would call that a charitable explanation for her behaviour."

"But your being away must have made it an easier decision for her — she had less responsibility."

"Colin! She never felt any responsibility for me. Good

God, she used to produce me like an exhibit at tea parties and before dinner but otherwise she took no real interest in me. Nicholas was the one she loved. We all loved Nicholas."

There was a sad silence while Colin gently stroked her hand.

"I'm surprised you loved him, if your mother apparently favoured him so much," he said at last.

"It was because he saw that I was left out. He remained unaffected by it all, and tried to compensate me. You wouldn't understand."

He restarted the car and drove on through the summer morning. But with every mile Sophia's realisation that she was going back to London caused her more distress. The wrench away from Needlewick had been too sudden but could surely not account for the extent of her depression. A week ago she had been quite content in her father's house, planning her future. What then? What was it?

Was it that her return to Needlewick and Helen's diary had given her a glimpse back into the brightly lit, albeit sometimes acutely painful world of childhood she had relinquished the second her foot touched the doorstep of home after her first Needlewick summer? Then, even as she crossed the threshold from porch to hall, she had known her mother was gone. She remembered her father's surprising embrace at the door, and Nicholas waiting on the stairs. After that moment there could be no return. It seemed to Sophia, now speeding home from Needlewick a second time, that she had briefly resurfaced into the light, but was about to plunge again into the murky depths of the pool her father had dug and stocked and tended for her by giving her an expensive but inadequate education, social training, and now a brilliant marriage.

Nicholas had told her on the first night that she would

be required to choose. They had sat together on her bed, not in it as they might have done a couple of years back, as he told her the history of the summer. While Sophia had been stumbling through head-high bracken, waking to bright, bird-noisy mornings, ploughing through musty novels in the dim Roundstones drawing-room, Nicholas had been laid up in bed, an innocent, necessarily passive witness to the final disintegration of their parents' marriage.

"You know she had started to go out a lot, you know we thought it was that man, well it wasn't, it was women. Meetings, marches, plans and committees. Father found out, a friend of his saw her one day. She told me, of course, she used to come to my room late at night — I was often awake because being in bed all day I didn't get tired, and she'd tell me all the excitement and jostle of the day. She used to say: 'You've seen me, Nicholas, you know me. Aren't I as good as you, or your father? So I must have a voice, we must all have a voice. I'll do anything for that.' But he called her a slut. I went down to the library for a book one evening and they were in the hall. He said if she ever attended any more meetings he would divorce her. She was beside herself. She shouted at him about a morality which allowed her to be a rich man's whore so long as it furthered his career, but stopped her going to meetings which would allow her to gain a little independence and freedom. And he started hitting her. Smack, smack, smack, smack, back and forward across her cheeks until her hair was torn down by his ring and the side of her face was bleeding. And she didn't resist but cried only: 'I gave up so much for you. Well, I won't do it again because there's no point. The difference now is I don't love you.' And that was it. The next day she left."

Smack, smack and her hair torn down. Beautiful, beautiful mother with her soft gleaming hair and thin skin. She took her fragile little body and wild dreams and threw in her lot with the suffragists because collective male brutality was more tolerable and easier to resist.

Sophia had seen her mother soon afterwards, in the Rose Garden in Regent's Park, at the end of the summer when the grass was sodden and the few remaining blooms hung damp heads and exuded a weary, sickly perfume.

Suzanna was waiting on a bench, wearing the heavy brown coat she normally used only for driving. Her hair was dressed in a business-like bun under a neat hat; old brown shoes peeped from beneath a defiantly flirtatious petticoat. Why does she have to dress so dowdily, what is the point? was Sophia's first thought, but, at the same time, her heart turned over at the futility of her mother's gesture, how characteristically she had spent much thought on her appearance, this time in an attempt at self-effacement, and managed only to give her beauty a greater clarity — like an old master in a plain frame. When they kissed, her mother's cheek was soft and fragrant as always. It was Sophia's weakest moment, but it passed the instant they moved apart to sit at a distance from each other on the damp seat.

"Mind your skirt, it's not very clean," Suzanna admonished, at once irritating her daughter. "I'm sorry we had to meet here — I wanted some privacy."

Sophia, whilst covertly searching her mother's face for signs of bruising, was awaiting an apology of a different nature.

"How is it at home?" Suzanna asked.

Sophia noticed that she was clasping and unclasping her fingers over the handle of her umbrella and was relieved that at least her mother felt some anxiety.

"What do you think?" she replied coldly. "It's hell without you. Father is furious."

"And Nicholas?"

"I thought you saw Nicholas quite often."

"I do, yes, but I think he puts on an act for me. He tries to be strong. I don't want to ruin his chances, he must work hard for the new term."

"Oh I shouldn't worry. He seems to spend all his time studying. And he'll be away in a couple of weeks." What about me, she cried inwardly, don't you care about me?

Her mother was gazing out over the gardens, her eyes averted from Sophia's face. "I had to see you, to make sure you understood, Sophia. And to give you a chance, if you want to take it." Receiving no response, she continued: "Nicholas did explain, didn't he, why I had to leave?"

"Not really, no. I don't understand you. I don't think he does, even."

"Oh he does, I'm sure. Didn't he tell you about your father?"

"Oh of course there was that. But why provoke him? He was bound to hate what you are doing."

Suzanna turned to her suddenly with such a pleading, desperate look that she almost softened.

"Sophia, don't talk like that, you sound so bitter. I had to do what I felt was right. He was trapping me — I'd just shut my eyes and ploughed on for so many years doing what he wanted."

"It was what you wanted!" Sophia exclaimed harshly. "You enjoyed every minute of that life."

"I thought I did at times, if I thought at all, but underneath. . . . Sophia, please! Don't let it happen to you. Don't give in to him. You must be free. I want you to have the chance. I'll give you this chance if you come to live with me."

"I don't even know where you are living," Sophia interrupted. Inside her head the shutters were slamming fast.

Don't offer me insecurity, poverty, question marks, dirtying of hands, mother. Don't. I don't even want to look.

"I'm staying with a friend for the time being. I have a salary from the Society, just a little, for the administrative work I do. You would carry on at school. Oh there are so many people for you to meet — and ideas, Sophia."

"I'm happy as I am, thank you."

"But I thought I was, all I wanted seemed to be your father and Nicholas, and you, and nice things and friends, but it's not enough. I can now influence things, the way people think. The world is changing, Sophia, for women in particular."

Sophia suddenly turned towards her mother and half raised her hand. Only the memory of other fingers which had left their mark on that cheek prevented her from slapping her face and saying: *Can't you hear how silly you sound?* But she kept silent.

For a moment Suzanna regarded her fearfully, but then seemed to relax as if the fight was over. Did she even look relieved for an instant? Quite calmly she asked: "Did you like Needlewick?"

"I don't think liking came into it. It's only a village. I miss my cousin."

"How was Eleanor Gresham?"

"She was well. She's a strange woman."

"Did you think so?"

There was a long silence.

At last Sophia got up. "It's very chilly here."

"Yes, yes, and I must go."

They embraced again, and this time her mother's cheek was cold and slightly salty. They promised to write, to see each other soon, but hurried away in different directions.

*

This time her father was out when Sophia returned home from Needlewick, so she and Colin had tea together in the drawing-room. Then at last he left her alone in the big, quiet house. A fire had been lit in her bedroom, doubtless on her father's orders, but this sign of his consideration only added to her sense of oppression. He's got me back again, she thought. Here I am, all ready to dress in my best and go down to dinner with him. On life goes.

At Roundstones now the tea things would be cleared away, her aunt would be underfoot in the hot kitchen helping with the dinner, and Sophia might have been lying on her narrow bed gazing out at a wide sky. But I was only a guest there, she thought sadly, I didn't belong. So in a miserable, numb state she dressed for dinner, stifling tears which had no apparent cause and a yearning which seemingly had no object.

But this suppression was highly dangerous, for the enforced intimacy of another meal with her father proved intolerable. Sophia, dressed in thin, oyster-pink lawn, shivered as she sat on the satin upholstered chair to the right of him. Pleasantries were properly exchanged; the Needlewick relatives were all accounted for, "And thank you, father for having a fire lit in my room, it was most thoughtful." She asked after his business, and then found nothing else to say. And she could take no comfort from the knowledge that she had only two more months until she could leave the house forever and be Colin's wife. *Father's face will simply be replaced*, she thought, panic-stricken.

Unexpectedly, certainly without premeditation, she heard herself say: "I've decided against marrying Colin. At least, I think I'll postpone it."

The words sounded so sane and natural that she was surprised by their impact on her father and had taken another mouthful of melon before she realised that he was sitting quite still, one hand on his napkin, another still holding his fork.

"I hope not," he said at last.

"Yes, I hope you don't mind." Fortunately she did not giggle at this last-stated wish, although having said it she was amazed by her impudence.

There was another silence. "Has Colin any views on this subject?"

"Oh, I haven't mentioned it to him. I haven't quite made up my mind." I actually only thought all this up in the last three minutes.

"May I ask why you have changed your mind?"

"There are various reasons, I think. I don't love him enough is one, I suppose. I think I'd make him pretty miserable, therefore. And I suppose I don't want to be married at the moment. I feel as if I haven't had a chance to live at all yet."

"Do you know how foolish you sound?" he asked suddenly.

"Do I? Are these feelings foolish, father?" Her voice wobbled. The prospect of his disapproval had always terrified her. Never had she given him such cause. She clutched at remaining shreds of control by completing her melon before quietly leaving the room.

Why, why, why, why, why, demanded her footsteps as she climbed the stairs. Oh Sophia, what have you done? For it was done. Colin might have softened her and talked her out of making any wild decision; her father's frigid affront only scored fierce lines under her sudden complete change of heart. It was done and, as he now would hate her, there was no point in trying to win him back, except of course by begging forgiveness for a temporary aberration and going ahead with her plans to marry as before. But having taken the plunge she could not go back. It had not been so terribly difficult, after all, to do the unforgivable. Sophia had always sensed that her father's power lay in his great charm and in his ability to withdraw it completely. She had known that almost anything would be better than incurring the full weight of his wrath. When she returned from Needlewick in the late summer of 1909 to be presented with a clear choice — his goodwill or her mother's unreliable care — she had chosen the former. Now she had neither.

She could not bring herself to speak to Colin either on that night or during their next meeting. In an absurd way it did not seem relevant that she was not after all intending to marry him. She realised that, as she had never properly engaged herself in communicating with him, she was accustomed to going through the motions of talking to him with her mind elsewhere; it would be going against months of habit actually to tell him what she was thinking.

She planned to write to him — eventually. Meanwhile her father subjected her to no pleading, no arguments, no rages. Only silence. An icy draught seemed to blow through the house. Sophia's hands and feet were always chilled as if she were physically unable to withstand such an absence of affection. At night she lay in bed with rigid limbs and sore eyes until too exhausted not to sleep. Only Nicholas might have protected her. But she had waved goodbye to Nicholas once too often.

Out of desperation she wrote at last to her mother, care of a relief organisation in Zurich, an address received from Suzanna at Christmas. She merely stated that she wished her mother well, and that, as she planned to terminate her engagement to Colin, she found she had no plans for her immediate future (she did not write: for her life) and wondered whether she might come out and join Suzanna for a while. And immediately after sealing the envelope she rushed off a note to Helen Callwood, offering to come to Cambridge. Unable to think of an excuse for writing, Sophia offered none. In her heart she knew that she sought Helen's forgiveness and, with it, comfort.

But she sent both letters with a kind of hopelessness, as if she were committing them to the depths of the ocean, almost certain that she was sending them into voids from which there could be no reply.

Still she said nothing to Colin. It was as if she was living at such a distance from everybody that whether or not she was engaged, or to whom, did not matter at all.

Simon Theobald was incensed by his daughter's failure to take action.

He was suffering dreadfully from the collapse of all his hopes for her, but she was apparently drifting on with Colin, putting off the moment of revelation; or had she merely been playing when she suggested that she might defer the marriage? Furthermore, enormous expense would be incurred if Colin was not told at once and the wedding later had to be cancelled or postponed. Twice he broke his silence to ask Sophia when she intended to inform her fiancé of her new plans and, receiving no satisfactory response, decided to speak.

He chose his moment with great care, watching the still-engaged pair consume an elaborate meal as far as the dessert before casually demanding: "And what is your response to Sophia's interesting new approach to her engagement, Kilbride?"

His would-be son-in-law as usual looked at him eagerly, delighted to capture his interest. "Sir?"

Sophia laid down her knife.

"I assume she's told you of the new arrangements." Theobald added lightly.

Colin's boyish gaze was now directed humorously at Sophia. "Let me guess. Gretna Green?"

Sophia took a peach and rolled it across her palm, enjoying the cool weight of it. Whatever happens now, she thought, the peach will still lie on my palm. Nothing so terrible will happen.

"We'll talk about it later. Perhaps," she said at last.

Theobald's fruit knife twisted into a grape and deftly removed two pips; one, two were scraped off onto the side of his plate. "My daughter is a cold fish, Kilbride, I believe you may well be glad to be shot of her after your initial surprise. In that respect she's very like her mother — you can never be quite sure what she's thinking. Best steer clear of a woman like that."

Colin still did not look like a drowning man, his voice held amusement and affection. "I think Sophia and I understand each other pretty well," he remarked.

"We thought of christening her Suzanna, but I decided not to in the end. Even then, when I had no cause to be suspicious of my wife, I felt I did not want to create another female in her image."

"I thought you loved mother very much then," Sophia said, her voice low and restrained. "You'd only been married a few years."

"Oh, love, Sophia! You're still such a child. I was always falling in and out of love, young men are like that, it's on their minds much of the time. I landed up with your mother, but it might have been any one of a number of young women; all beautiful, blooming and smooth-haired."

"Then why choose my mother? Why choose her, to uproot her and bring here?"

"It was the challenge, Sophia, the challenge. She seemed so fixed, so gloriously a part of her home. I

—132—

thought, let's see if I can do it. Let's see if I can make her mine."

Colin made an ill-judged intervention. "Needlewick seemed a very pleasant little place, I thought."

"Yes, you might even have spent part of your honeymoon there. That would have been much the best plan. Then Sophia need not have gone on her own, and it would have been too late."

"Sir? Too late?"

"Kilbride, a pleasing little analogy has just come to mind. Forgive me, Sophia. I think Needlewick is like some kind of diseased whore — it leaves its mark on anyone who dares penetrate it. Christ, Suzanna was rotten! And look at my daughter now!"

The peach had fallen back on the plate and Sophia's hands were now folded on her lap.

"What my father's trying to tell you, Colin, is that I've had second thoughts about our engagement. Nothing definite. I just think we should talk about it, perhaps postpone it for a while."

"I see."

"Perhaps, if father would excuse us, we could go now. I'd like to talk to you alone."

"Let the boy finish his meal. Give him a few more moments' pleasure."

Sophia stood, waiting expectantly for the men to rise and for Colin to follow her from the room.

But Colin stayed in his chair and, as Simon reached for the port, Colin slowly lifted his hand to offer his glass.

13

HELEN'S REPLY WAS remarkably prompt — Sophia identified the round, girlish handwriting at once. Helen wrote very briefly that there was no need for Sophia to go to Cambridge as she had an engagement in London at the end of the month and would call one morning. Sophia wrote back with much more warmth saying how delighted she would be to meet her again.

During the ten days she had to wait for Helen no word came from her mother.

Her father, as expected, showed no sign of softening. He had never relented towards Suzanna so Sophia presumed that he could, if necessary, maintain this air of intense disapproval towards her for the rest of his life. She made a point of waiting until she knew he'd left the house before going in to breakfast, and he frequently dined out. When they did eat together they rarely spoke but listened to the sound of each other's chewing and swallowing. Any conversation Sophia tried to instigate was met by polite but monosyllabic responses.

Once she embraced him. They were alone for a moment before she left the dining-room; she put her arms around him and murmured: "I'm sorry I've caused you so much pain, father." He sat rigidly until she had withdrawn her arms and then said: "When it's convenient perhaps you will let me know the new date of your marriage, or whether you've decided to call it off completely."

She had planned her pathetic little gesture since the early hours of the morning and his rebuff was crushing. But still she could not hate him sufficiently to break free of him; she had been dependent on his goodwill for too long.

She met Colin by making an appointment at his Chambers, for he was never at home when she called.

She knew his rooms quite well, and while waiting for admittance had cause to wonder at the difference one conversation at dinner could make. In the past, when meeting him here, he would have been hovering at the window, watching for her, even when with a client. Hurrying awkwardly along the uneven pavement outside, she would always look for him and wave. That afternoon she was kept waiting for several minutes, although she had been punctual, and when he at last ushered her in, he seated her firmly in the chair opposite his desk, and himself behind it, not, as formerly, drawing up a stool and sitting at her knee so that he might reach forward to kiss her cheek or hand once in a while.

She had not anticipated that her rejection of him would cause him such obvious hurt. Formerly buoyant, rather schoolboyish, unashamedly and openly affectionate, he was now very composed, closed down, neatly dressed, hair tidied, face pale. He had retreated far inside himself to lick his wounds. It was only on recognising this that she fully realised the enormity of what she had done. She did not blame herself for breaking the engagement — it was entering into it so selfishly in the first place that now seemed to her so culpable.

While they exchanged initial courtesies he watched her

intently, as if she were some dangerous zoological specimen; his eyes were narrowed, his expression wary.

At last she said: "I came to apologise for that dreadful dinner. It was unforgivable of my father to have interfered in that way. It must have seemed to you appallingly cruel."

"I had to know. In fact I have been wondering when you would have broken the news otherwise."

"I don't know, I couldn't bring myself to," she replied miserably, hating herself for the lie, but how could she admit he hadn't been important enough. "It all seems so unreal, even now. If you asked me what I really wanted I wouldn't be able to say, or why I suddenly became unsure of my own mind. It's so silly, isn't it?"

He would not respond to her appeal. Taking his fountain pen, he turned it over and over.

"Colin, I'm so sorry!" she exclaimed. "I didn't want to hurt you like this!"

He shrugged: "That's all right."

He had retreated so far that again the enormity of what she'd lost, what he would have given her, struck her. So much generous, undemanding love. "Oh Colin, I would have been no good for you," she said, "you're too fine for me."

She had succeeded at last in angering him.

"Whip yourself with that if you like. You know it's nonsense. The thing is you don't love me and never have."

"Do you want us to finish completely?" she asked.

"If you like. It's up to you."

"Please don't say that. Please. We're in it together, of course we are. Shall we just postpone our decision for a few weeks? What do you think?"

"What's the point?"

"So we can be sure we're doing the right thing. It seems so dreadful to throw it all away."

—136—

"If you like — you can let me know what you want in a few weeks."

"And you? You must let me know — you have every right to let me know. Your feelings might change too."

He rose abruptly, helped her with her coat, and showed her to the door.

Life at her father's house was intolerable. Sophia's nerves were constantly wrenched by her relentless, circular mental processes. Where should she go? What should she do? Why had she so carelessly destroyed her future with such a good man?

She went daily to her writing box — formerly her mother's, it was small and impractical but had a lock and key — and from it she lifted her sheaf of Needlewick photographs. They had been badly taken, and, caring little for them after they were developed, she had crammed them together so that their edges were crushed. But now she held them up, one after another, and studied them as if in them she might find comfort and hope.

There was one of Mrs Gresham, her face so ill-defined that she might have been any woman in any garden. The photographs of Roundstones were better: here were her uncle and aunt and Helen, who was smiling. Remembering the diary, Sophia could not gaze long at that smile. Those of the clearing held no magic. She had photographed the woods wildly, too impatient to focus the lens, and too inexperienced to attend to the light.

Yet she loved to handle the photographs. They were to her as precious as even a shopping list written in a beloved hand is to a lover. The photographs were a direct link with Needlewick.

She recognised through them that there was only one place where she might rest, collect herself, even find counsel. She wrote to her Aunt Margaret of the post-poned engagement and asked whether she might return to Needlewick for a little while to think clearly about her future.

Helen came on a cold, blustery day that might have presaged autumn had the roses in the garden not been so bright and fragrant. Remembering how her cousin loved flowers, Sophia filled the vases in the drawing-room with early chrysanthemums. A light, plain lunch was ordered. She spent an hour selecting and discarding clothes as being either too showy or too expensive and finally chose an old cream dress she'd not worn for years. It reminded her of summer days in the war. She disliked the dress but it seemed right for Helen's visit.

The diaries and photographs were laid on her bed. Sophia thought that after lunch they might go up and look at them together. Perhaps Helen would laugh at her old fantasies and former intensity. How else could she be asked to forgive the past?

Helen came at eleven precisely. Sophia stood by the window and listened to the murmur of voices in the hall, quick steps on the stairs, the opening of the door. "Miss Callwood, Miss."

"Helen!" Sophia crossed the room, took her elbows and kissed her cheek. "How lovely to see you. Please, sit down. Your jacket?"

Helen was very composed.

"No, I said I'd keep it. I can't stay long."

"Some coffee?"

"No, thank you."

"Nothing at all?"

Helen had retained the ability to be very still. Sophia poured coffee for herself with shaking hands, her care-fully prepared conversation now useless. For want of anything else to say she exclaimed: "I like your hair, a bob suits you.'

In fact Helen looked terrible; the short hair only accentuated the roundness and pallor of her face. She had been plump as a girl, now she had the figure of a matron and her calf-length brown skirt revealed thick ankles and heavy shoes. Even her eyes, now hidden behind thick spectacles, seemed to be those of a complete stranger.

Sophia had expected to find her cousin reserved but she began to talk in a calm, friendly manner: "It's much easier to manage shorter hair when one has so little time."

She was examining the flowers, porcelain, loose covers. "It's a lovely room."

"Yes, I've always liked it. Of course, everything is terribly old. We've hardly changed it since mother left."

"How is your mother?"

"Oh, when I last heard she was well, I believe." Shame spread a hot blush across Sophia's cheeks. "I'm not very good at keeping in touch with her. She travels so much. I was glad to find your parents in good health when I was staying with them."

"Yes, they seem all right. I don't have much opportunity to visit them any more."

"Tell me about your work, Helen. It's such a mystery to me. I never thought you'd be interested in mathematics."

"Oh, what did you think I'd do?"

"I don't really know, but you seemed more artistic." Phrases of your diary sing through my memory night and day, she thought.

"Yes, well it's more useful to be practical. I find the mathematics a great challenge."

Her tone was not rude or repressive but Sophia was chilled. Helen talked as if to a passing acquaintance, a fellow passenger on the train.

"And what's it like living in the university? It would

frighten me to be among all those great brains."

"I suppose I felt daunted at first but one gets used to it. I'm in my element there."

Your element! Sophia cried inwardly. Oh, Helen, what about the Tunnel Woods, the cow parsley in the lane, the girl with no hat who made daisy chains and raced sticks in the stream?

"Don't you miss Needlewick at all?"

"At first I did, I suppose, but not now. There's nothing for me there, you see. And of course Mrs Gresham's death was a great blow. I always liked seeing her. I could have got nowhere without her encouragement."

"I wish I'd known her better. She seems to have been a remarkable woman. Everyone in Needlewick misses her so much."

"She was the one who particularly wanted me to go to Cambridge. You know she would have gone there herself if she hadn't started to be ill."

"I didn't know that," Sophia murmured.

"No, she didn't tell me for years. Anyway, now she's gone I'm afraid I don't have a lot in common with anyone at home." There was an uncomfortable pause and then she asked: "What about you, you're engaged, aren't you?"

"Was, I was. Now — we're not sure."

She shrugged. "Oh, what do you do now, then?"

"What do you mean? Oh, well, I have so much housekeeping to do." Sophia's words fell on the air like farthings from a piggy bank. What did she do? What had she done?

"You must feel the loss of Nicholas."

"Yes. I do."

"I should have liked to meet him."

"Would you? I didn't think you knew much about him."

"I always envied you having a brother."

"Yes, I miss him dreadfully. He was a dear. He somehow managed to stay close to all of us when the family split up, you know."

"It was a wicked war!"

Sophia looked at her in surprise. "Why do you say that?"

"Well don't you think so?"

"No, I don't." Sophia had never judged the war at all. Suddenly she asked impulsively: "Would you like to see his room?"

Helen looked astonished: "Yes, if you like."

"No, no, of course, how could you possibly be interested? Anyway, there's nothing there, we cleared it all away. There wasn't much to tidy, he was terribly organised."

"Please — I'd like to have a look."

Sophia's skin was prickling with embarrassment as they mounted the stairs. This wasn't in the least what she'd intended. And of course, when she opened the door, the room looked so ordinary — an over-tidy bedroom in a large town house. She felt Helen must be confounded.

But Helen walked confidently into the room and sat on the bed. "There's a great dearth of young men at Cambridge," she said. "There must be so many empty bedrooms like this one."

"Yes, I suppose so."

"Did he write to you much? I remember he was always writing when you were staying with us."

"I think he tried to protect me too much, then, and during the war. His letters were so cheerful always. But because he never wrote about how it really was I suppose in the end I was shut out. I'd rather have known. I felt when he died I didn't know him properly at all, but I might have done if given the chance. That was part of the loss."

"Of course." Sophia noticed her glance covertly at her

watch. "I'm meeting a friend for lunch at one."

"Oh, I imagined we would have lunch here." Nothing of importance had been said, the time was slipping through Sophia's fingers. "I'm sorry it's been so long since we've been in touch."

Helen smiled politely.

"It was really Mrs Gresham's death that made me write to you," Sophia said desperately.

"Yes, I had imagined there was some connection."

"You know she left me your diary."

"Yes, she said she would." There was no hint of confusion or self-consciousness, merely a little grimace. "I shudder to think what I'd written."

"Don't you remember?"

"Not really, no. I expect a whole lot of stuff about you. I remember keeping a diary during that time you came to stay. I was so thrilled you were coming."

"I would have thought you'd have hated me reading your private diaries."

"I haven't really considered the matter. It all seemed so foolish. I couldn't understand Mrs Gresham, but it would have been churlish to have refused. Her letter asking my permission seemed so anxious and urgent, quite unlike her, and I could tell by the writing she was far from well."

"But I upset you so much!"

She laughed. "Did you? I expect I was jealous. You must have seemed very exotic to me. I think you were probably good for me. I know I couldn't stand Needlewick after you'd gone. I had to get away, it seemed so parochial. I went off to school. The Greshams were terribly kind and helped with the fees."

"That was very good of them."

She rose to her feet and walked to the door. "Anyway, I'm afraid I really mustn't be late. My friend would be rather annoyed."

"Helen, what about the Tunnel Woods? Did you ever go back?"

"Go back?"

"Don't you remember what happened? That's why I wanted to see you. I read the diary."

Helen was on the stairs and did not falter. "Well, of course I remember the Tunnel Woods. I went for walks there sometimes, though I wasn't supposed to. I don't know when I last went, it's quite a way. I got lazy."

Her gloves were on. She was by the front door.

"Would you like to have the diaries back now?"

"Good Lord, no! I should throw them away if I were you. I couldn't bear to read them."

In a moment she'd be gone, she was turning away.

Suddenly she took her spectacles off and polished them with a handkerchief. Briefly her gaze met Sophia's and for that moment Sophia saw a glimmer of the remembered Helen in her dreamy grey eyes, once lit by an unreachable inner candle.

"I hadn't realised you were short-sighted," Sophia said.

"I am, very. I didn't realise myself 'til I went away to school. I must have lived in a blur for years. I'm surprised no-one noticed." She extended her hand to Sophia. "Goodbye. Thank you for writing to me."

"Goodbye." Sophia closed the door behind her. The hall was dim and silent. Helen's visit had made no impression there.

"I am going back to Needlewick, father."

No reply.

"You don't mind?"

No reply.

"Have you any message for Aunt Margaret?"

No reply.

But Sophia no longer feared him. She was cut off from

—143—

him and from everyone. A little fragment of gossamer, she was floating up and away, and , if he caught her, would she care?

"I still haven't heard from mother, though I've made several enquiries and written to a forwarding address."

At last he laid down his knife and fork.

"Why do you wish to speak to your mother?"

"She is my mother. I have neglected her long enough. It is inexcusable of me." His blue stare had its customary effect of making her say far more than she had intended. "And there was a diary, you know, left me by Mrs Gresham. I wanted to ask mother about her childhood in Needlewick and a place called the Tunnel Woods."

The Tunnel Woods. The name fell into the great chasm between them and created another silence. But as Sophia left the room she glanced at him and saw that the skin beneath his eyes was wet.

14

M RS BUBB HAD been taken ill. She'd had a stroke. She required constant nursing. Margaret Callwood wrote that Sophia would have to postpone her intended visit to Needlewick.

Sophia tore up the letter, took the first available train to Cheltenham and from there a cab. She had no other choice. She had burnt all her boats in London — if Needlewick too was burning, as it were, then so be it, she would rather go down on the Roundstones' ship.

During the journey she thought mostly of Helen to whom she had extended such a warm hand of friendship. She could not but feel hurt by Helen's casual behaviour after so many years. Sophia had certainly wronged her cousin in the past, but surely now they were both adults they might be friends. Had Helen no need of her, no residual love or admiration?

Of Colin she had seen nothing since their meeting at his Chambers. Her initial anguish at his suffering had been replaced by a great weariness. What could she do about it? She obviously did not have the ability to make anyone happy, being so unhappy herself. She found herself envying purposeful Helen with her ink-stained fingers and myopia; she might be a blue-stocking but at least she had knowledge and a congenial occupation. What am I, thought Sophia, but a former fiancée, former sister and, to all intents and purposes, a former daughter?

But as the train neared Cheltenham she became preoccupied with more immediate problems and frightened by her audacity at travelling to Needlewick expressly against her aunt's wishes. She wondered what she would do if she were turned away, though she knew such dramatic action by her mild uncle and aunt was unlikely. For once she welcomed the slow drive to Needlewick though her courage dwindled with every twist in the lane. Not wishing to give her relatives an excuse for sending her home at once, she dismissed the cab at the bridge in the village and walked up the hill, carrying her own bags. By the time she arrived at Roundstones rain was falling in soft, heavy droplets and she had to struggle with both luggage and umbrella. After ringing the bell she stood dripping forlornly in the porch for a considerable time before anyone responded.

Aunt Margaret could not disguise her horror at the sight of Sophia.

"Oh my dear, didn't you get my letter?"

"What letter, aunt?"

"I wrote several days ago. Surely I posted the letter. I can't have you here, Mrs Bubb is sick, the house is all upside down. One of the Makepeace girls. . . . but she's so lazy. . . . and there's the nurse to feed. I can barely manage."

"Oh, I'm so sorry. Oh dear!"

"Well come in now and I'll make some tea. How did you get here?"

She peered hopefully up the lane for some means of transport to carry her niece away.

The drawing-room was chilly and unused. The garden

stood still in the rain, the roses well past their best bloom. Despite her aunt's letter Sophia had hoped for long cosy gossips, solitary rambles, a gradual recuperation from all the emotion of the past month. There would be little rest here, she now realised, for she was an intruder. But she could not leave.

Her aunt was completely absorbed by the current crisis. On Sophia's previous visit Margaret had been attentive and sympathetic, deeply interested in her life and welfare. Now she could think of nothing but Mrs Bubb. The tea was weak and there was no cake.

"We'll have to see what your uncle says. He might be able to run you back to the station."

"Oh, I couldn't ask him to do that."

"Perhaps Mr Gresham. He's very good."

"Look, aunt, if you can bear it, I'll just stay here for the night, and then in the morning I'll make my own arrangements. But don't worry, please. I'm dreadfully sorry to intrude on you like this. I knew nothing of Mrs Bubb or of course I wouldn't have dreamed of coming. But I promise I'll be no trouble. I might even be of some help."

She was regarded without hope.

"Is there nothing I could do?" Sophia asked.

"Well, perhaps you could sit with Mrs Bubb while I get on with the supper. Susan Makepeace really is so unused to the kitchen still, and the nurse is very particular about her food. She usually has a break about this time."

As they climbed the two flights of stairs to Mrs Bubb's room Margaret whispered: "I asked if she'd like to be brought downstairs but she seemed to be agitated by the idea. She's occupied the same room since her husband died about thirty years ago."

"You're very good to her, you really are."

"Sophia, she's been with my family since she was

twelve. This is her home. Nothing can be too much trouble."

The room was very close and smelt of sick, old flesh. It was small and bare — Mrs Bubb had collected few belongings over the years.

"We think she can hear and see," Sophia was told, "but she can't speak or move so we're not sure."

When told that Sophia was to sit with her for a little while, the large mound on the bed made no sign. She was turned every half hour or so, and now lay on her back with her eyes closed. Sophia perched herself on the hard chair by the window and gazed anxiously at the still figure.

Frightened, she turned away and was startled by the view commanded by this second floor room. From under the eaves of Roundstones one could see west along the valley of the Needle for several miles, even perhaps as far as the Tunnel Woods — yes, there were woods away in the distance. Sophia's gaze followed the line of the river — she could even, in places, make out the path.

And being at the corner of the house there was another, larger window which overlooked the garden, Middlecote Hall and, away to the east, Needlewick. Mrs Bubb had the most wonderful outlook. Sophia wondered how often she had been watched unnoticed from these windows.

She moved across to the bed and looked fearfully down into the housekeeper's face; the eyes were now open and seemed to stare directly up at Sophia who smiled uneasily. Mrs Bubb made no response except perhaps for a slight flicker of the steady gaze. She was lying on her back, and the heavy flesh around her mouth and nose fell back, leaving the mouth slightly open, ugly and fleshy with a dribble of saliva at one corner.

"I hope you're comfortable," Sophia murmured and returned to her chair. "Perhaps next time I'll bring a book," she added more confidently, "and read aloud to you."

The patient's silence was intimidating but Sophia continued: "I was so sorry to find you were ill. My aunt wrote to me but I didn't receive the letter." The words sounded over-loud and hollow in the still room.

There were no books except a red-bound Bible by the bed. A few photographs stood on the mantelpiece and the ugly chest-of-drawers, too far away for Sophia to study, and too near the bed to be approachable.

Instead she gazed at her hands and feet, the hem of her dress, flecks of dust on the old carpet; the room was so neat and clean it afforded little other distraction. She tip-toed again to the bed but crept away because Mrs Bubb now had her eyes shut.

At last, after little more than three quarters of an hour, her aunt returned and ushered her out.

"Your uncle's here and will be up to have a look at her in a while. We've put your bags in your room — supper should be ready quite soon. It was really very kind of you, dear."

After hurrying downstairs and closing the door of her room behind her, Sophia gave a nervous little giggle. She was shivering uncontrollably for her room was cool after the warmth of the sickroom.

Yet she would stay and do it again if need be. She might even perhaps be of use to her aunt. This was such a novel idea that she laughed out loud.

Harry Callwood actually encouraged Sophia to continue at Roundstones, perhaps motivated by the fact that during the very plain evening meal Margaret was far more flustered than usual and appeared to be over-strained.

"I'm afraid the potatoes aren't quite cooked. Oh — is

the meat tough? She doesn't understand the oven yet. She tries very hard but in some ways she's like the mother." She paused and then addressed her husband. "Sophia says she can get a cab in the morning."

"Oh, aren't you staying?" he asked mildly.

"Harry, she can't! I've so much work. I'm so sorry dear, but Mrs Bubb takes up all my time."

"I'd like to help," Sophia said tentatively.

"There now, I think that would be a jolly good idea," exclaimed the doctor. "We'd hoped Helen might have come home but she's writing an important paper, she says. Sophia could be a great help, Margaret, and she'd perhaps brighten us all up."

"But Sophia can't cook or clean," Margaret cried, forgetting her usual deference. "What could she do?"

"I can sit with Mrs Bubb. I can help with the house. I have lived through a war, you know."

There was a tiny pause as these last words made their impression. The three at table had not lived through a war — they had lived beside a war as bystanders. But the phrase had its due effect.

"Of course, dear, but are you sure that's what you want? Is it the best thing for you — your father, and then your engagement, we were so sorry. . . . such a nice man."

Sophia knew that her aunt did not want her there; she regarded her as an intruder, and did not believe she could be of any help.

To prove her worth she insisted on clearing the meal alone. Too tired to resist, Margaret went quite willingly to rest in the drawing-room. The Makepeace girl was in the kitchen, large and pale with her mother's huge, protruding eyes. She had been eating her own meal and sat indolently at the table, pushing her spoon round her bowl. The kitchen was so untidy Sophia could not think where to begin.

"I'll clear the table. You fill the sink and make a start, Susan."

Neither of them spoke again. Sophia considered that when she had tidied the dining-room she had done enough. "We'll have coffee when you've finished," she instructed the servant, and fled.

Coffee never appeared. When Sophia returned later to the kitchen Susan had gone, leaving the room moderately neat. Sophia went to bed. Sleep came easily in Needlewick with only owls to disturb the quiet of the night.

15

SOPHIA MANAGED TO develop a relationship with Susan Makepeace. With plenty of admiration and encouragement the girl worked quite fast, and Sophia spent some time each day chivvying her round the house.

Occasionally Sophia went shopping for her aunt, and once a day, in the late afternoon, she sat with Mrs Bubb. She dreaded these times, but regarded them as the fee she must pay for being allowed to stay in Needlewick. She learnt the tasks of turning the patient and giving her little dribbles of water. Within a couple of days she was allowed to sit in the sickroom alone from five to seven each evening. Her greatest fear was that Mrs Bubb might either die or speak while she was with her and, to avoid either eventuality, she asked her uncle if reading aloud to the patient might be appropriate. She had a superstitious belief that no-one could die while she was reading to them. There was very little of interest in the bookshelves at Roundstones, but eventually she chose a thick volume of Grimm's fairytales, very closely printed and with macabre pen and ink illustrations. Thereafter, whenever Mrs Bubb had her eyes open, Sophia read stories to her, one after another in a slow, clear voice. She created a vicious world in that sickroom, of blood falling on white flesh, of old fairies and giants, dark forests, noble princes and talking beasts. She never knew what Mrs Bubb thought of these stories, or even if she heard them. Sophia found them fascinating.

Visitors came frequently to Roundstones. Lady Middlecote called daily, as did the new vicar, a loud-voiced, helpless churchman with red skin and thin mousy hair. Margaret had many friends in the district, which rather surprised Sophia at first, but she reflected that her aunt had grown up in Needlewick, a doctor's daughter, and was now a doctor's wife and so of course would have innumerable acquaintances. Sophia received a good deal of praise as she handed the tea cups: "So kind of dear Sophia to come and help her aunt." Always there were polite enquiries after Helen — unspoken were the words: "She should be here to help." Nobody mentioned Suzanna.

Sophia had plenty of time to herself, indeed the days seemed very long. She walked and read, but did not much relish her own company. In the end, for want of other occupation, she took to writing to Colin long letters, full of village gossip and fairy tales. At first she received no reply and indeed expected none, but after a while he began to write brief little notes from his office or from court. Sometimes he drew sketches of brother lawyers or ushers. She began to watch for the post, but was disappointed even when there was a letter from him. She craved affection, not pen-sketches. She examined his signature, "Yours, Colin". He had always before written "With all my love". She also wrote dutiful little notes to her father to maintain a fragile link with him.

On Friday evening Mr Gresham called to ask if she would like to take a walk with him the following day. "I thought you might be lonely here," he said, with his usual diffidence. Sophia accepted eagerly, although she was intimidated by his grief for Eleanor. She was so starved of companionship that she would gladly have accepted an invitation from almost anyone. Besides, she liked him and found him very kind.

At her suggestion they took the path to the Tunnel Woods. She was irresistably drawn to them, and frequently walked that way alone, though never far.

They began by speaking of Mrs Bubb. It was a safe topic and a natural one.

"Do people normally recover from strokes?" Sophia enquired, sweeping the leaves of the willow with her fingers as they strolled past. The prognosis of Mrs Bubb's illness was a forbidden subject at Roundstones.

"Your uncle would know better than I. I think age, weight and general health have much to do with it."

He was dressed smartly in a light summer suit. Sophia, suddenly visualising him alone in a gentleman's outfitters, felt her heart contract. He was such a small, unassuming man; how could he choose himself a suit?

"My aunt is so fond of her, it'll be a terrible blow if she dies."

"Yes, well of course Mrs Bubb knew your aunt when Margaret was a baby."

"Did you ever meet my grandparents, Mr Gresham?"

"I do remember them, your grandmother in particular. Eleanor always said Suzanna was very like her mother. I think the little girls were left to Mrs Bubb a good deal."

Sophia became aware that he was performing a dance behind her in an attempt to take the side of the path nearest the river. She made room for him and said, "I find it rather frightening to sit in the room with poor Mrs Bubb. She is so quiet, yet I feel she knows a lot about me, from when I was here before."

"I expect she does. And she was devoted to your mother."

"Oh don't say that, Mr Gresham, everyone seems to have been fond of my mother. I feel now that I scarcely knew her."

She realised, too late, that he would probably dislike her display of emotion, but he replied softly, "Of course, I did not know her very well, and only briefly before her marriage. But you could never forget her, never. And Eleanor used to talk about her very often."

He spoke his wife's name calmly, and in reply Sophia adopted the same unsentimental tone. "It's always puzzled me why they didn't keep in touch if they were such good friends. I mean I would have thought Mrs Gresham would have been sympathetic to mama when she left my father."

"Oh my wife was deeply attached to her. Deeply attached. She was very sad when Suzanna went away from Needlewick. Suzanna scarcely ever wrote to her. I think maybe that's why she gave you the diary. For your mother's sake."

Sophia was surprised that he should mention the diary after his reluctance to discuss it before.

They had come to a part of the river where the water trickled softly round large smooth rocks. Although the day was overcast and rather chill she suggested they might sit for a while.

"I used to come here with Helen. I told her off for dabbling her feet in the water. It was considered so unfashionable to have brown feet."

It was peaceful by the river with Mr Gresham. He had an air of tranquillity about him that day, as if the shyness and distress which she had seen in him before had withdrawn to reveal an inner core of strength.

So she dared.

"Mr Gresham, you know the diary, you said you read it. Helen wrote about 'her people', do you remember? And I was cruel, I laughed at her. But something about

—155—

your wife, I just wondered, did she know about the Tunnel Woods, where we used to go? You see I don't understand. Before I read the diary I couldn't think why Helen tried to deceive me by inventing all that stuff. I knew it must be more than just to impress me. And then, meeting her recently, I felt she didn't care one way or another as if none of it meant anything to her. So I came back, because I couldn't understand how she could have forgotten."

Her words tumbled about them. He was perched uncomfortably on a large boulder, bare-headed. Watching his face she realised suddenly that he had come because of the diary and his wife's knowledge, and had been waiting for this moment.

"Eleanor wanted to go back to the Tunnel Woods," he said, "but by the time she told me it was too late. I could not get her there on this rough path in her weakened state. It was too much for her. So I went one day by myself, having by then read the diary."

"Did you go to the clearing?"

He smiled. "I tried, but I couldn't find it. There was the path, and the Tunnels, but then, once away from the Tunnels, there seemed to be no way through the bracken, none at all. I presume because Helen had stopped going there it had become overgrown."

"Yes." Her voice was faint with disappointment.

"You see, it was because of those woods that your mother fell out with Eleanor, or so Eleanor always thought."

"Why, why? Did they go there too?"

"Oh yes, they all went. They were quite a little gang. Oh, I didn't live here when I was a boy but I remember meeting this group of girls at Christmas parties. There was your mother and your aunt, and the Henshaw girls, now Lady Middlecote and her sister whom you met recently, Deborah Parditer, and Eleanor. Eleanor was always the odd one out, as you can imagine, but she and your mother were very close. Eleanor kept notes your mother had written her when they were little girls. They had their own code. She made me destroy them before she died."

The river flowed clear and untroubled, and a bird flew swiftly from the opposite bank. Minnows flicked from under the rocks. "Their friendship must have been hard for Aunt Margaret," Sophia reflected.

"Yes, I think so. She loved Suzanna so much. I think they all did. I think even I fell for her a little on the brief occasions I met her."

More than twenty-five years of river had flowed past these same boulders since Mr Gresham had last seen Suzanna. Sophia had photographs of her taken during her engagement; she was always dressed in white, with masses of fair hair piled above her delicate neck.

"So why did they fall out? It seems so sad. I think mama must have needed her friends so much over the years. After all, her family hasn't exactly stood by her." Sophia was suddenly gripped by such pain and remorse and longing to see her mother that she could not remain still. She leant forward and trailed her hand in the water.

"They found the clearing. All of them. They used to roam about the countryside together and one day they found the clearing and after that nothing was the same. Your mother changed. She became secretive. She took to going off on her own. Finally, after much persuasion she confided that something had happened in the clearing and she had to go back there often, alone. She never said what for. Eleanor was very bitter at being excluded. I imagine the Henshaw girls were also upset but they were slightly older anyway, nearly ready to come out. And your aunt and her sister became very close because your aunt was prepared to go with Suzanna as far as the

Tunnels and wait for her."

"My aunt knew?"

"Oh yes, she knew."

"So she must have understood about Helen? Or did she?" But before he could reply Sophia noticed that John Gresham's knuckles were white with cold. "Mr Gresham, you're frozen. Let's go back. It's so cold here by the river."

They walked rapidly, she deeply concerned for him in his light suit; he was so slight, though he denied being cold.

"What do you think was in the clearing?" she asked.

He shrugged. "Who knows? Perhaps nothing except childish secrets."

She sensed that he had disclosed all he would or could, so they spoke of other things, even, briefly, of Colin. He of course knew of the changes in her plans and expressed his sympathy at her predicament. "We're very friendly still," she assured him. "I write to him almost every day. But perhaps we won't marry at all." She tried to appear cheerful and offhand.

She asked him her last question as they neared the little path which led up the hill to Roundstones. "Mr Gresham, when I last saw you I felt you wouldn't want to talk about the Tunnel Woods, or Helen's diary. Why did you change your mind?"

"I thought Eleanor would have wanted it. And I've been thinking about you, Sophia, and whether you were made sad by the diary. Perhaps that's why you came back."

He said goodbye and turned away towards the footbridge but suddenly changed his mind, took her hand and kissed her cheek.

She remained by the willow some time, but gradually uneasiness made her hurry towards the house. She had recalled the cold eyes that had so often followed her progress along the path by the river. Sure enough she heard a rustling behind her and Michael appeared.

"Oh for heaven's sake!" she exclaimed and began to run.

He followed her easily. "I wondered when you'd like me to take you to the woods," he suggested. "I was there, remember."

16

ONLY THREE WEEKS after the end of her previous visit Deborah Parditer returned to Needlewick. It was much too interesting there for her to stay away. How quickly events had moved: Eleanor's death, Sophia's visit, Colin, a broken engagement (for which Deborah took some credit having expressed doubts about the impending nuptials), and now Mrs Bubb with a stroke. Wretched woman, how like her to pick on an illness which would be as protracted and inconvenient to poor Margaret as possible. And to top it all Sophia had come back to Needlewick. Deborah was rewarded for years of intimacy with her Needlewick friends by being accepted into the fold without question at this time of trouble.

On the evening of her return she went to visit John Gresham, as was her wont, although such calls were an ordeal for both. He felt swamped by her energy and enthusiasms, she confused by his academic pursuits and barely concealed desolation. But beneath the awkwardness was much love, nurtured through years of quiet afternoon calls, mutual care of Eleanor and respect for differences.

He answered the door himself and ushered her into the

sitting-room where the evening sun poured across the light furniture, and ruthlessly revealed the smears on the window panes.

"Is that woman looking after you, John?" Deborah demanded, noting also the dust on the occasional table by the fire. "They'll always take advantage of a single man."

"I feel comfortable with her," he replied — not a satisfactory answer.

They drank sherry and discussed Mrs Bubb's illness.

"You're to stay well clear of that house, John. You've had enough of invalids."

"Oh I'm not needed there. You knew of course that Sophia has come back to help?"

He rose suddenly and went to the window, the sherry lapping dangerously in his glass.

"Not much use, I'd have thought. Doubtless she's here more for her own convenience than Margaret's. Still, at least she's a bit of young life. I don't suppose there's been any word from Helen?"

"No, I think not."

"It seems so callous. Has the girl no feeling? Doesn't she remember how devoted Mrs Bubb was? Oh, I remember them so clearly together. You'd meet them in the post office, baby Helen clutching Mrs Bubb's skirts. You'd find them walking together in the lane. I never knew how Mrs Bubb had the patience."

"Children quickly outgrow their early affections."

"Margaret never did," Deborah responded tartly.

Mr Gresham now removed a letter from his inside pocket.

"This came yesterday. I haven't mentioned it to anyone else yet. It's addressed to Eleanor. It's from Suzanna."

"No! Surely not!" Deborah had to hold herself firmly in check. The letter was inches from her hand. She spoke

—161—

calmly. "I assume you've read it?"

"Of course. Please, I feel you should too. She wants to come back to Needlewick and asks Eleanor for support."

There was Suzanna's handwriting on the envelope, very small and untidy, the letters ill-formed, yet still familiar. Deborah had preserved all the scraps and notes she'd ever received from Suzanna, or had salvaged after they had been discarded by her.

"You'll need more light, it's difficult to read," John said.

Dearest Eleanor,

I've been thinking about you more and more, what a long time since I wrote, since I saw you. How are you? Is your health improved? I do think of you though I'm not much good to you, am I, or anyone, I sometimes think, not really here, I get so tired now. I wrap food and do the parcels for the refugees but often they come undone. Everyone is very patient but I keep thinking of Needlewick and how quiet it is there, not like here with all the people and foreign languages. I'm so tired, Eleanor, I work so hard and get nowhere, as usual.

How are you and what about dear John? Lucky Eleanor. I should have stayed in Needlewick, too, with the sun on the river, not come away. Sophia is not after all going to marry her great catch. Poor Sophia, what must she have gone through, I shall come at once and bring her with me to Needlewick — will Margaret be able to put us up, or could you if it's too much for her? A girl needs her mother and I will support her of course. I wish I had been strong enough to do the same but I was in love with Simon then and nothing could have stopped me marrying him.

And on the way home I shall visit Nicholas's grave. I've seen pictures of the cemetery — it looks so tidy don't you think, all those neat stones like dominoes, push one, I think when I look at the photograph, and they'll all tumble down, one after another on to the grass. I wish you could have been there at Nicholas's service. I thought all the time if Eleanor had been here I could have held her hand. I needed you, Eleanor. The others came and kissed me but were such a long way away because of course they did not know my Nicholas. Nobody knew him. How could he have been my son, beautiful boy, so good. I don't know how he could have been my son and so fine.

They are encouraging me to go home and will pay my fare because I have no money. I give all Simon's allowance to the Relief Fund because of course he would hate to know it went to foreign refugees and I would not touch it, poison money.

Oh Eleanor, July in Needlewick, so green and quiet, and the sun on the river. Your garden will be lovely at this time of year I think and remember. Will John have his old white hat on while you are reading this? And you will be washing raspberries and redcurrants and pressing them into a summer pudding? Shall we go for walks or are you still too weak? Eleanor I'll sit with you and tell you about my adventures, poor little adventures, and bring you strength though I haven't much to give, which is perhaps why I'm writing at last because I know how you must feel.

I'll come then, tell Margaret I'll write soon.

While Deborah read, John Gresham shuffled uneasily about the room, but came to rest near her chair and gazed tenderly into her face as he saw that she had reached the end.

"It's a sad letter, isn't it? She doesn't sound like Suzanna."

Deborah spoke on an indrawn breath in a vain attempt to hold back tears. "No, no, it doesn't sound like her at all. I thought she was so immersed in all that work. She was such a prominent figure during the war. Poor Simon, do you remember how hopping mad he was over those pacifist rallies?"

"It seems Nicholas's death must have affected her very badly. It's only natural."

"Yes, yes, of course. *I* was there at the service. She was very pale, I remember, and in a great hurry to get away. She seemed not to want to speak to anyone, least of all to Simon, or Margaret, or even Sophia." Oh Suzanna, she thought, I was there, I would have taken you in my arms; I knew how you loved your son. But you barely gave me a glance. I went there for you, but as usual you did not want me.

"More sherry, Deborah?"

"Perhaps, yes, just a drop."

"I thought, anyway, I must write and tell her again about Eleanor's death. And of course she can't stay at Roundstones with Mrs Bubb ill."

"Jane will put her up," Deborah offered, but there was an awkward pause as they both had a mental picture of Suzanna in Middlecote Hall.

"Have you told Sophia?"

"No, I've not seen her since this came."

"How is she?"

"She seems quite well, perhaps a little subdued."

"She must be wondering what the future has in store for her. Really, that family seems to be doomed to unhappiness. What precipitated the end of her engagement?"

For an instant their eyes met.

They both knew.

17

THE GRIM ROUTINE at Roundstones continued, a great strain on Sophia in particular, for she stumbled along on the periphery, quite dispensable and therefore by no means absorbed by the drama.

She had developed devices for making her daily session in Mrs Bubb's room more bearable, and had established a mode of speaking to the patient which satisfied her; politely, intimately, as if Mrs Bubb were indeed the cosy, genial confidante she had never been in good health. Sophia imagined her words soaking through the housekeeper's skull to the red tissue of her brain and hushing and shushing their way into the woman's consciousness somehow, but there was never any outward sign of response.

Having made the gesture of patting the bedclothes, Sophia would settle herself at the window. "I hope you don't mind but I've brought a letter from Colin to read. Amazingly enough he is still writing to me, despite the cruel way I ended our engagement. It makes me think sometimes that all that was a bad dream. I certainly enjoy his letters."

Each time a letter arrived from London, Sophia

opened it with the same jolt of anticipation. Would this be the love letter she at once longed for and dreaded? Dearest Sophia, think again, I love you, I miss you, come back to me. I need you . . .! Depending on her mood Sophia responded to this imaginary letter either with a sad refusal or by ordering a taxi, speeding back to town and falling into his arms. Lying in her lonely bed at Roundstones, she often tried to visualise what it would be like to sleep next to Colin, letting go completely. She would turn her head on the pillow and imagine him lying beside her, reach out and put a tentative hand on his hair. How strange to have a man there.

But his letters were always a terrible disappointment. Devoid of any mention of how he felt, they contained long amusing accounts of court cases, evenings with friends, anecdotes. Once he made an allusion to her father whom he had met for lunch. "He is obviously very lonely, and sorry about what has happened, but I'm afraid unrelenting towards you. I told him I thought you'd done the right thing and behaved quite properly, but he would not be softened. He did say you were quite at liberty to return home."

Sophia dwelt on this last sentence for some time, wondering if it was actually a concealed plea from Colin, but no, she thought, if he really wanted to see me he could always come to Needlewick. But then her reaction when he had last made a surprise visit had scarcely been one of welcome and he would probably therefore not risk another rebuff. And she could not invite him to come because she mistrusted her feelings. She was afraid that, if she saw him, she would experience an immediate rebirth of the old irritation, and then she'd be trapped, because she could scarcely summon him to Needlewick simply to check that she still did not love him enough to marry him.

Once a letter was read and pondered over, it was time to check the prone figure on the bed. Was she wet or dirty or dry-lipped? No, quite all right. "There you are, Mrs Bubb, you're all tidy." Then Sophia would wonder away for a re-examination of the ornaments and photographs which by now she had studied intently. One, a copy of a print she had found tucked away in the nursery cupboard at home, was a stiff family group of her grandparents and two small girls: Margaret, serious and stolid, and Suzanna, slight and, even in that faded picture, eye-catching with her fine light hair and the suggestion of a naughty smile. Another photograph was taken in the garden at Roundstones, a family at tea on the lawn, so distant that Sophia could hardly make out her uncle and aunt with baby Helen. There were two wedding photographs (Suzanna and Simon Theobald, and Harry and Margaret Callwood) and one of Helen, perhaps a year or two younger than she had been during Sophia's first Needlewick summer, standing alone in the garden with her startled eyes shadowed by a big hat. There was one more picture, so blurred that Sophia wondered why it had been thought worth retaining, of two girls, probably Suzanna and Margaret, perhaps on the lawn at Roundstones. They stood in middle distance on grass but their forms were so indistinct they were scarcely recognisable. There were no momentoes of Mr Bubb, nor indeed any indications that Mrs Bubb had a family of her own at all.

On the afternoon following her walk with Mr Gresham Sophia asked Mrs Bubb about the Tunnel Woods. She spoke softly and intimately, as befitted the sharing of secrets.

"I wonder if you can tell me anything about the Tunnel Woods, Mrs Bubb? I went that way yesterday."

Sophia moved her chair closer to the bed. The patient's face was turned aside slightly, her eyes were closed.

"Of course you know I used to go with Helen. You must have seen us many a time."

The room's silence was intensified by the cacophony of birdsong from without.

"And then of course my mother went there often, Mr Gresham said. Were you ever there? Were you?"

Suddenly Sophia reached out and placed her hand on Mrs Bubb's cheek to turn her face. She stroked the warm forehead fiercely in an attempt to open the eyes.

"What was there, Mrs Bubb? Do you know? Did they tell you?"

Sophia approached her mouth close to the old woman's ear. "My people," she whispered, her own hair brushing the pillow.

And then, becoming aware of her proximity to the white linen sheets and the sick woman's half open-mouth, so close that a residual heat of exhaled breath reached her cheek, Sophia recoiled and moved to the window.

After a moment she said brightly: "I'll read to you then, shall I?" She picked up Grimm and began to read aloud. She failed to notice for several paragraphs that she had chosen the same story as the day before.

On Sunday she walked towards the Tunnel Woods. Her aunt was in no state to care whether or not her niece chose to accompany her to church, but for form's sake Sophia had been to Communion at ten o'clock. Even the church held excitement for her now — in this very pew had sat her mother and Margaret, and there the Henshaw girls, making signals perhaps at Eleanor Carney, demure and elegant between her parents. Sophia noticed that Deborah Parditer was back in Needlewick looking as alert as ever. And there was dear Mr Gresham — Sophia caught his eye and gave him a shy smile causing his face to dissolve in a boyish grin and lose for a moment its habitual solemnity. Sophia wondered what the vicar had been like in her mother's time; the current incumbent was a terrible bore and spoke at length on the theme of Bread in the Wilderness. She did not listen for long but wondered instead what secrets had been whispered in the dark porch after Communion services. Had her mother, sitting here on Sunday mornings, longed for the heavy Sabbath luncheon to be over so that she could hurry and skip along the path to the Tunnel Woods? Today no such obstacle stood in Sophia's way for Sunday lunch, like every other midday meal at Roundstones these days, was cold. Nobody minded when Sophia said she would picnic on her walk.

She sat, to eat her lunch, on the same boulder in the river, made lonely by Mr Gresham's absence. She had never before met anyone like him. Such quietness and kindness were rare. She knew that he would never judge her or dismiss her, whatever she did. He had looked so lonely and inconspicuous in the Gresham pew but Sophia suddenly wondered how the vicar dare preach so dry and unimaginative a sermon before a man of Mr Gresham's intellect.

Her solitude was so oppressive that she was not quite as dismayed as usual to find herself watched by Michael. She looked up and saw him crouched on the bank, chewing a blade of grass.

"You've changed your mind then, I see," he remarked.

"About what?"

"About going to them woods."

"No, I haven't. I just thought I'd bring my lunch here to have a bit of peace and quiet."

"Oh, too noisy for you up at the house, is it?"

She did not rise to this sally but said mildly: "I expect you're sorry to learn Mrs Bubb is so unwell. You must have worked with her for some years at Roundstones."

She had no idea whether he and Mrs Bubb ever spoke to each other in those days when he had worked for her uncle. She did not remember ever having seen him in the kitchen though he must have eaten there. She was a little surprised to realise that she had angered him.

"The old sow's got what she deserved!" he said venomously. "Always spying on people."

Sophia was tempted to respond that this seemed to be a common fault among the servants at Roundstones but said nothing.

"Are you coming then?" he demanded.

Sophia found that the short discussion of Mrs Bubb had somehow confused her. For a moment she and Michael had been on the same side and she did not feel as repulsed by him as usual. And she *was* eager to see the clearing again.

"Are you sure you can get into the woods?" she asked.

"Oh yes. I go there often." He reached out his hand to help her off the boulder. "Come on then. It won't take long."

She ignored his proffered help but jumped back on to the path and began to walk towards the Tunnel Woods. She was quite frightened, in a nervous, anticipatory way, but more of the prospect of being disappointed than by the nature of her companion. And the gusty breeze and warm air had sapped her energy; she felt too lethargic to resist. The Tunnel Woods were an irresistable lure.

They scarcely spoke. He soon overtook her but stopped occasionally to check her progress. His gait was awkward, jerky, hurried as if, she thought, he was excited.

"How often do you go the woods?" she asked.

"Oh often. Good poaching territory."

"You remember the clearing where you surprised Helen and me?" she asked reluctantly. She had to be sure.

"Oh yes."

"I suppose you often followed us there."

He did not reply but it seemed unlikely that he was silent out of shame. He was breathless, and wondering if he was perhaps asthmatic, she called: "Do you want to slow down?"

He stopped so abruptly that she walked into him. He pushed her gently away. "I'm all right."

She was shaken by the unexpected physical contact. Her fear was no longer suppressed by excitement at the prospect of seeing the clearing again. She had just collided with the body of a muscular, full-grown man, not a rather puny boy.

After a moment she said: "I think it might be a little too far for me today. Perhaps another time. I have to look after Mrs Bubb, you see."

"Go on. We're nearly there. See!"

And indeed they were very near the closed entrance to the woods. "Yes, so we are. I'll perhaps just see how you get in. I don't think I'll go all the way to the clearing today."

But she was already helpless. She had waited weeks, perhaps years, to revisit the clearing.

When they reached the woods he turned away from the river and walked along by the fence. Then, where nettles and grasses seemed to grow strongest and tallest, he suddenly did a sideways, crab-like movement and disappeared from view. When Sophia reached the place she found him holding brambles aside for her. Behind him a little square of fence had been cut carefully away. Once they were through Michael moved confidently among the dark trees. She followed cautiously, wary of tearing her stockings, and found to her relief that they soon reached a well-marked path.

"Is this the way to the Tunnels?"

"That's right. Clever, aren't I?"

As they walked she searched for familiar landmarks but remembered no individual tree or twist in the way. Overhead the sky was now completely overcast and the woods were dim and dusty. She had forgotten how steeply the path climbed away from the river and how narrow it was in places. But she had not forgotten the Tunnels.

They came upon the entrance so suddenly that Sophia had no warning until she realised that Michael had halted and was waiting for her. "Here we are," he said.

"I think I'll just wait to get my breath back before I go on. It's quite a climb, isn't it?" She could not imagine why she had come so far with him for she knew now that it would be impossible for her to plunge into the darkness beside him. It had been bad enough with Helen holding her hand, and even then. . . . Sophia remembered that terrible game they had played when she had been left to stumble alone down the echoing Tunnel.

"I've often thought there must be a way over the top," she remarked conversationally. "I remember Helen once said these Tunnels were only built as follies."

"Oh yes, you can get over the top. How do you think I managed not to be seen when I followed you?" He brought his face up close to hers. "There's nothing to be afraid of, you know. These woods are quite ordinary. Not even that big. I know them well."

The skin on his nose was large-pored. She could smell his sweat and his breath, surprisingly sweet.

"Oh well, let's go over the top then."

"No, that would take far too long. It's much further that way."

"It would be much more interesting for me. I've only ever been through the Tunnels."

"As I remember, you were always pretty afraid of them."

He'd seen it all then.

"I'm glad I didn't know at the time that you were watching us."

He did not comment. "Come on then. I'll hold your hand. You'll be all right."

"No, I won't come. I'm sorry, Michael. I'm tired. I've had enough. Some other time. I must get back. Mrs Bubb."

"You've got plenty of time. Come on."

Too late she perceived the extent of her danger for when she turned away he clasped her wrist with his thin strong fingers.

"Michael," her voice quavered and pleaded.

"Come on, you little bitch. Come and see the Tunnels. Come with me."

She tried to twist and wrench her hand free but he suddenly changed his grip to her upper arm and then swung her round to hold her fast with his two hands. "Frightened, are you? Frightened of little Michael, the doctor's boy?"

He was backing into the Tunnel.

"Frightened of a poor boy who dared to give you cheap scent."

"What do you mean?" The darkness was closing around her.

"You threw it away. I found it in the hedge. It cost me a lot, the ticket that won me that."

"But I was only a child. I'm sorry."

"Only a child, yea. Are you still a child? Are you? With your dainty little shoes and silky clothes?"

Suddenly he twisted her back against the Tunnel wall. Its unyielding dampness was almost a relief. At least it was solid.

"All right. We won't go to the clearing. We'll stop here and have a bit of fun. You haven't had much of that, have you?"

It was very dark. She could scarcely see him at all,

only very dimly his eyes. And it occurred to her that he was an expert at this game; she could imagine him ripping screaming rabbits from snares. His hands were expert hands. One hand he moved from her shoulder to her neck, forcing her head back and up so she could no longer speak without pain. He pushed his knee between her legs, his body hard up against hers. She could move her hands but was weakened and pinioned by his hold on her neck.

"What shall we do then, eh? Talk together like you and that gentleman friend? You liked talking to him, didn't you? Didn't get much else done did you? Poor chap. I felt quite sorry for him. It never pays to be too much the gentleman, though, does it?"

Had she been able to speak she would not have screamed or pleaded with him to release her. A question had suddenly dropped clear and demanding into her head and was awaiting an opportunity. *What else did you see in the clearing*? is what she would have asked. But the pressure of his hand on her neck had made her faint. She was supported only by the forward thrust of his body.

The blackness of the Tunnel came inside her head. His voice was very distant. "I preferred you when you used to have your hair loose on your shoulders. It swayed with the hem of your dress." He pulled at her hair with his free hand. Pins dropped down the neck of her blouse. "Lovely hair. I remember your hair. You used to push it back, like this, and flick it from your shoulders. It was your way of showing it off. I touched it once as you hurried away from me. You'd never speak to me, would you?"

He stroked her hair gently, rubbing it between finger and thumb, then began to run his fingers across her face.

"I watched when you sat in the field over the river, you and her. I watched your mouth, always opening and shutting, telling her tales. Sometimes you smiled and I wanted you to smile at me, but you never did, not properly, only laughing."

His fingers probing the skin near her nose smelt of the woods, of green things he'd pushed aside. His finger tips were hard but his touch was gentle.

"All I had of you was the odd sight of your petticoat, or the flick of your hair in my face. But I remembered the smell of you when you went away. I dreamt about you coming back and me getting you like this, here, you see, where you couldn't get away. So I could show you."

He was stroking her lips, teeth and chin.

The pressure of his hand on her neck was released a little as he moved his fingers from her mouth to join his other hand at her throat, holding her neck quite softly in his two hands. Then he leaned forward and put his lips to her ear. "You could have bitten me, I gave you the chance to get away."

His taut body moved against hers in a spasm of excitement and fear.

"You won't forget me again, little bitch. You've stayed in my head. I've waited for you. Well I'll make you remember me. I will." He was breathing so hard that when he moved his lips through her hair, across her cheek to her mouth his kiss was interrupted by the need to gasp for air. He kissed her, and his breath was sweet and soft. Her mouth fell open in surprise and his tongue darted against her teeth, the roof of her mouth and back across her lips. His hand moved from her neck to her breast; with finger and thumb he stroked it softly, felt for the nipple and squeezed, then his fingers edged across her stomach before unexpectedly cupping her hard between her legs. Her head shot back and his mouth fell on her chin. For an instant she listened to the pulsing of her body, then, sensing his weakness, pulled away from his warm hands and ran.

She stumbled out of the Tunnel and down to the river. The newly erected barrier no longer posed a problem for she simply plunged knee deep into the water and waded along by the bank until she could climb back on to the path. She ran on, her feet soaked and her dress heavy about her legs. All the time she cried, not for herself but for Michael whom she had treated with contempt one last, shameful time. Knowing her strength she had laid the bait, allowed him to give her a paltry measure of excitement, and then run. And all for one, wet-lipped kiss and strong hands in a dark tunnel.

Entering Roundstones by the kitchen door she met in the passage Susan Makepeace who informed her that Mrs Bubb had made a sudden turn for the worse; "and that Mr Gresham was here asking for you."

"When, when was he here?"

"A few moments ago. I've just shown him out."

Sophia hurried through the hall and out of the front door.

"Mr Gresham! Mr Gresham!"

He was not in sight but she ran along the lane and caught up with him near the gate where she had first seen Michael. "Mr Gresham!" When he turned to face her, she realised how extraordinary she must look with her hair tangled down her back, her dress drying in stiff, muddy creases around her calves. She stopped short.

"I've just got back. I heard you called."

There was a moment's recognition in both of them — for an instant they were caught off balance by this confrontation, as if the ostensible reason for seeking each other out had been pushed aside and the much simpler desire to be close was without doubt. He took her hand and led her to the gate where they stood, with her untidy head resting against his neat shoulder. A kiss so light that she could not afterwards be sure of it fell on her hair.

"I was so sorry to learn about Mrs Bubb," he said at last. "Of course I would not have called had I known."

"What happened? I didn't stop to ask."

"A second stroke, I believe, about an hour ago."

"Is she all right?"

"She's still alive."

Each had a hand on the rough, warm wood of the gate. The field at which they gazed sloped upwards in rough tufts and hillocks, trampled and pitted by cows which now clustered together under trees in a far corner. Early evening in August, and the sun was already casting deep shadows.

"I came to show you this."

He dropped his arm from her shoulder, and handed her Suzanna's letter, withdrawing a little to allow her some privacy as she read. Her hands trembled as she carefully unfolded the paper but she read steadily and without obvious emotion. He was aware of her habitual restraint, and how unlike her it had been to come running after him up the lane, and he again felt the quickening in his blood at the sound of her voice.

"This must have been hard for you to read," she said at last. "I can't understand why she thinks your wife is still alive."

"She seems confused, don't you think?" he suggested gently.

"Her letters are always muddled, though, the few I've had. They're usually a great jumble of ideas and experiences."

"And it's very hard to read her writing which used to be so clear. I showed this to Deborah Parditer. We both think your mother seems ill and distressed. I think you should not therefore rely on her coming, Sophia. And if she does come she may not be very strong."

"Yes, I see. Yes. I know I can't depend on her." She was ashamed of the tremor of self-pity in her voice. "Well, thank you for showing it to me."

"I think we can do nothing until we know what her intentions really are."

"No."

They stood on for a moment looking over the gate across the field until Sophia said at last: "I may be needed. Thank you for calling, Mr Gresham."

They shook hands, laughed a little and parted.

18

WATCHING OVER MRS BUBB was now much more of an ordeal. There was no question of reading Grimm; it seemed to Sophia that it would have been irreverent to pour fantasy into the ear of one so close to death. She was apparently completely unconscious, her eyes were always closed and the colour had drained from her face and hands leaving the skin a pale yellowish grey, as if slowly the blood had seeped away from these extremities to concentrate all its efforts on keeping her tired heart pumping.

Sophia could no longer wish anything but that the woman would die. What point was there in breathing when she could not think or speak or feel? Sophia took books and sewing up with her, but found she could do nothing but watch minute by minute for the moment of death. The suspense was nerve-wracking.

Outside the sickroom the house was running more smoothly. Margaret had obviously resigned herself to the loss of Mrs Bubb and had begun to pick up the threads of the household. Susan Makepeace was a sulky but quite intelligent girl. She would perform all her allotted tasks and then sit in the kitchen with her hands folded, waiting until told to do something else. Once she was found to be dependable enough to arrive on time in the morning, it had been decided that she could live out, and each evening at eight she hurried away down the hill to the village. Sophia had never made her once intended visit to Mrs Makepeace. She felt exposed by the fact that Susan cleaned her room and washed her clothes; those big Makepeace eyes missed nothing. But her aunt seemed pleased with Susan who must have seemed malleable and willing compared to the stubborn Mrs Bubb.

The trickle of calls had ebbed a little as Mrs Bubb's condition stabilised, but they gradually increased in volume as news spread of her relapse. Everyone, it seemed, wanted to be sure not to neglect a dying woman. But actually no-one came to see Mrs Bubb, all were Margaret's friends come to support Margaret in her trouble. They acted almost as if she were dying too — or as if she needed tending like a fragile flower whose prop is about to be torn away. Sophia didn't believe Aunt Margaret was fragile and was impatient with answering polite, sorrowful questions.

Deborah Parditer called. Knowing the Roundstones routine as well as the inhabitants themselves, she came when the nurse was resting and Margaret with the patient. She wanted to speak to Sophia.

The afternoon was fine and they sat on the terrace where Sophia felt less intimidated by her visitor. Susan served them quite daintily with tea; she had become expert at setting the tray and cutting thin bread and butter.

Mrs Parditer said officiously. "You're poor Mrs Bubb's replacement, are you, dear? What's your name."

"Susan, Madam."

"Susan?"

"Makepeace."

"Ah, a Makepeace girl. Well, I expect you're doing well. And you're very lucky to have found such a good position with dear Mrs Callwood. How is your poor mother?"

"All right thank you."

Susan retreated to count her blessings leaving Sophia alone with the inquisitor.

"It's such a pity about the garden," was Deborah Parditer's first remark, "it's amazing how everything seems to slip when there's sickness."

"The garden always seems delightful to me."

"Well, I expect you're not used to much by way of gardens in London." She paused for a moment, and then said: "I expect John showed you the letter from your mother."

"Yes."

"You've heard nothing else?"

"Not a word."

"Well, we'll see. I don't envy your uncertainty, but I expect you're used to your mother's vagaries."

"They don't affect me much. I've scarcely seen her since she left home." Sophia was irritated. It was surely no business of her visitor's.

Mrs Parditer now sat back in her chair and eyed Sophia curiously. Her victim took a bite of sandwich, frantically searching for a new topic of conversation. But it was too late.

"I admire your mother, Sophia. She has so much courage. She has always gone her own way and tried to do right. Her life since leaving your father can scarcely have been easy."

"Most people say she was foolish and unwomanly to give up her family life to work for the suffrage."

"Yes, well leaving your father did seem very rash at the time. But I remember when I heard I wasn't surprised. No, I seem to have expected it. Your mother was never one to be tied down. Your poor aunt used to try but even as a girl Suzanna was always off on one wild scheme or another."

"But you can't have expected her to leave my father. Surely no-one could have foretold such a thing."

"Oh, of course we all thought it romantic when your father came and swept her off her feet like that. You can imagine how we girls used to sit up late at night gossiping and speculating. We had nothing better to do. The whole district was agog with it — the romance of the rich Londoner and the local doctor's daughter."

Sophia sat up. She suddenly realised that in Deborah Parditer she had found a fertile source of information. She poured more tea, cut more cake, and asked casually: "How did they meet?"

"By chance. And after that he wouldn't leave her alone. He called or wrote daily until she had agreed to marry him."

"He's never recovered from her going."

"Hasn't he been tempted to marry again?"

"They've never been divorced."

Mrs Parditer seemed undeterred by Sophia's stiff response. "And he wasn't a man ever to sympathise with her cause, so it was a double blow. She couldn't have chosen anything more wounding to him. He was the very last sort of man ever to condone the idea of women having power."

"What about all the rest of you here, what did you think?"

Deborah was pleased to give her opinion. "Those women did some pretty extraordinary things — your own mother — sticking safety pins in tyres — so extreme and wild and sordid, I used to think. The idea of ladies in prison! And then in the war she did all that marching for peace and tried to remain friendly with the German women. We couldn't accept that, we were terribly patriotic, of course, and hated the pacifists. I couldn't understand Suzanna going along with all that, she had always been so strong-willed and clear-minded. I decided that she must have been indoctrinated. But lately I've begun to feel she might, after all, have been right."

"Do you?"

But Mrs Parditer had finished her tea. "Shall we stroll down to the river before I go up to see Margaret?"

She picked up her capacious bag and they walked slowly across the lawn, Deborah pausing occasionally to point out some flaw in the border. "Yellow roses are always a mistake. They look blown and faded almost before they're fully out. . . . I'm surprised at your aunt for allowing the mignonette, it's such an untidy plant."

Sophia unlatched the garden door for her and she stood looking out over the valley towards Middlecote Hall.

"And what about you, Sophia, what are you going to do with yourself?"

"I don't know. I'm needed here."

"Your aunt could manage perfectly well without you. She's very efficient, although she must be feeling that woman's loss pretty badly. It's always a mistake to be too dependent on one person."

"How do you mean dependent? Isn't one always dependent on one's servants?"

"My dear, from the moment Mrs Bubb arrived, the entire family relied on her to a ridiculous extent. Your grandmother was hopeless, she simply couldn't be a mother to those girls. She managed to produce them, but that was it. She could never settle, never focus on them properly. The poor things would have been terribly neglected were it not for Mrs Bubb."

"I could never warm to Mrs Bubb when I was a child. She seemed to hate me."

"Oh, she would. You weren't Suzanna, you see."

"My father accuses me of being like her," Sophia said with a sad laugh, suddenly in need of comfort.

"Well, there is much to admire in Suzanna. But of course she lacks stability."

Sophia's heart was beating very fast. For once she did not try to defend her mother, but asked: "Why do you think she and Aunt Margaret are so different?"

Mrs Parditer took her arm and leaned on her heavily as they walked down to the river. "Poor Margaret, she was younger, plainer, she played safe. Mrs Bubb sheltered her, kept her at Roundstones more. But Mrs Bubb would not, or could not hold Suzanna. Young girls are vulnerable, Sophia, easily influenced. Your mother had a very odd few years here in Needlewick before she married your father. She became isolated and took to rambling about all over the place by herself. I'm afraid we all rather gave up on her in the end. So in some ways it was a very good thing your father turned up."

"Why do you think she got like that, though?"

"I've no doubt you've heard plenty about all that. Oh, there were wheels within wheels. Fanciful girls. I kept my own daughters under a very tight rein. In that way, of course, Suzanna is right to do all her shouting and running about demanding decent education and responsibility for women. Girls need to have their heads filled same as boys, otherwise they pack their own heads with all kinds of nonsense. What nonsense is your head filled with?"

"None, I hope."

"We'll go on the bridge," she announced. "Why did you terminate your engagement to young Kilbride? Nice chap — I thought."

Sophia was startled by the directness of the question, but answered nonetheless: "I suppose I don't love him."

—184—

"Well, that's reason enough. You don't want to make the same mistake as your mother."

"But she loved my father."

"Yes. She was desperately in love at first. But she was also completely enchanted by the world he offered her — the escape from Needlewick."

"But you said she was so happy here. You said she loved the countryside."

"Did I say she was happy? And she didn't *love* it here. She was mesmerised. Haven't you ever wanted to join any of your mother's causes?" Mrs Parditer was not to be distracted from her main line of enquiry.

"It has occurred to me, just recently. I wrote to my mother. But I don't know. I don't feel very passionately about anything."

Mrs Parditer sighed and turned restlessly away from Sophia. "Yes, you're a typical product. A bright girl with nothing to do and no skill but an eye for a well-cut frock or a handsome man, and suddenly you find neither is enough. We were lucky, you see. We never expected anything else, but women like your mother have destroyed all that. Women will never have peace of mind again. They won't knuckle under. You're sure about Kilbride?"

"Oh heaven knows!" Sophia replied irritably.

"Well, if I were you I'd find myself an alternative occupation fast or you'll go and do the wrong thing out of sheer desperation. But don't go overboard like your wretched cousin. She's another one who's got very strange."

Mrs Parditer turned back towards the house and walked more swiftly up the path.

Sophia, seeing her chance slip away, called: "Do you remember the Tunnel Woods? What happened there? Tell me, please!"

"I never knew and now I don't think it much matters.

Yes, we went along the Tunnels, and we found a clearing, a lovely place, very quiet, almost circular. And Suzanna said afterwards she had to go back. I don't know why. She would never let anyone except Margaret go with her again. At first we asked them about their visits, but neither would reply. I know that Margaret was always told to stay outside the Tunnels. I used to think of her there, waiting for Suzanna. I never liked those woods. We thought Suzanna was being very selfish and childish. Why? Why do you ask?" She was still ahead of Sophia. She slowed her pace to listen to the answer.

"I went with Helen. And I'd love to go back, just to see." Sophia, distracted by the memory of her own last visit to the woods, faltered. "I've walked that way. But it's all fenced up. Did you know? I can't imagine why anyone would want to do that."

Mrs Parditer was now waiting by the wall, watching her. "What do you mean?"

"Well, how odd of the owner to go to all that expense."

Mrs Parditer's hand was on the latch of the garden door. She stared at Sophia in astonishment.

"But surely you know who those woods belong to now? Your father bought them as a wedding present for your mother."

19

MRS BUBB DIED in the early hours of a late August morning. After all the waiting, it was strange to find that nothing much had changed; there was only a general sigh of relief that she had at last gone. For that day at least Sophia could be properly helpful by writing notes and planning the funeral collation. She did not go up to see the body but was deeply troubled by its presence in the house. When she went to rest in her room after lunch she could think of nothing but the lifeless torso upstairs and the way slippers had lain slightly crooked under the washstand for so long, waiting without hope for their owner to shuffle into them. When, for relief, she got up and looked out into the garden she immediately imagined Mrs Bubb gazing at the same view day after day, year after year.

In the afternoon a few flowers came, but of course none from any of Mrs Bubb's relatives.

"Did she have no family at all?" Sophia asked her aunt.

"There was her husband, of course. They had a house in the village but she still worked here. He died before they had any children. Consumption, I think. But she belonged here. She was glad to come back."

Margaret seemed to have accepted the death calmly, but several times in the afternoon Sophia heard her go upstairs to the housekeeper's room. She looked dreadful in black. It drained all colour from her hair and face until both were a uniform grey. When Sophia suggested that mourning need not be worn she was rebuked sharply. "Sophia! She was my very dear friend. I owe her so much more than this."

"But you were very good to her. She was fortunate to have such a comfortable home."

"No, Sophia, it was she who provided a home for me."

By the evening all arrangements had been made and the proper people notified, including Helen who responded to her mother's telephone call by saying she would come at once. The day of the funeral was fixed — and beyond that, for Sophia, was a terrible blank. Her uncle had actually pronounced that he would like a holiday. Soon Roundstones would be empty.

After dinner Sophia took the path down to the river. The sun was setting behind a thick bank of cloud, the sky above was a faded golden blue and all the trees on the opposite side of the valley were etched darkly into the hillside. There was no light on the river, only shadow. The willow hung quite still.

She had not walked towards the Tunnel Woods since that shameful time with Michael and did not now, though she no longer feared him. She had not seen him since that day and sensed that he would not attempt to touch her again. That night she planned to walk over the footbridge and up the field path to the church. She was tempted to call on Mr Gresham but, on reflection, decided such an action was out of the question. She dared not approach him in the quiet of the evening with Mrs Bubb dead and the sun setting over Needlewick.

At the bridge she halted. Down the field towards her slowly walked a woman dressed in a long brown coat and heavy hat and carrying a clumsy bag. Sophia could not see her face but knew her and waited for her, unable to form a word of greeting.

"Sophia, is it you?"

Suzanna laid down her bag on the bridge to embrace her daughter, who was hurtled back to her childhood by that faint, familiar perfume which assailed her the instant their cheeks touched — her mother in a rustling pale gown kissing her goodbye before departing for the opera or a reception.

Sophia at last put her hands on her mother's shoulders and held her close.

"I didn't expect you."

"I got your letter. I wanted to be home. How's Mrs Bubb?"

Had she come only to see that woman?

"I'm afraid she died this morning. I'm awfully sorry."

Suzanna did not seem to hear but held on to the wooden rail of the bridge and gazed upstream.

"It's so long since I was here. Perhaps even before you were born."

Overhead white streaks of cloud swam over the blue. A bird sang clear and cold from a tree by the river and the water flowed quietly beneath their feet. Suzanna stood quite still, watching. Sophia noticed that the sleeve of her coat, in any case too heavy for a summer evening, was very worn.

"Have you come far today?" she asked softly, and then as Suzanna turned dreamily towards her exclaimed: "Oh you look so tired!"

"Yes, I am tired. I'm very tired. I need a little rest. They told me I did. How's Mrs Bubb?"

"I'm afraid she died this morning."

"Yes, I thought she would die. She must have been

very old. And what about you? I was so surprised that you should come here. I didn't think you'd like it. You didn't last time you came, do you remember, when you were a girl? You wrote all those letters to me, so brave, such a brave little girl but I knew you were hating it."

"It's nice. I like it now. It's peaceful."

"Yes, it's peaceful here though terribly poor still, I must go to the cottages in the morning. I thought it would be all right to come back. I need a holiday. I haven't had a holiday for such a long time, not since Nicholas died really."

"Shall we go up to the house, mother? Aunt Margaret will be very pleased to see you."

"I ought to have written, she never used to like surprises. But I didn't have time. They thought I should have a little rest. But it's not really fair on Margaret. She's got enough on her plate. How's Mrs Bubb?"

Sophia was so afraid that she could scarcely stoop to pick up her mother's bag and draw her away from the river towards Roundstones. This woman was so terribly unlike her bright, quick, beautiful mother. She was vague, nervy, all her movements clumsy, fumbling like a sleepwalker. Why does she not listen to my answers? Sophia thought. Why did she not show more emotion at seeing me? What about Aunt Margaret's reaction to this new, uninvited guest?

Suzanna paused several times on their way up the hill and turned to look back over the valley.

"It's peaceful here," she murmured, "so still. I should have come back before."

"Yes, I find it restful after London."

"I never really liked London though I thought I would. I was glad to escape from here. But this is where I belong."

The open French windows and lit drawing-room were a relief after the dark garden and Sophia thought that perhaps the brightness would restore her mother to normality.

But Suzanna stood blinking at the window.

"Nothing changed, nothing changed," she said.

"Oh, it must have done! I believe Aunt Margaret had new loose covers only a couple of years back. Look, you sit down here, mother, and I'll make some tea and bring Aunt Margaret."

She did not sit, but moved softly about the room. It struck Sophia suddenly that only her slender ankles were unchanged — they at least were still elegant.

She went in search of her uncle whom she met on the stairs. She told him that her mother was come but seemed strange, perhaps exhausted. As she spoke Sophia realised Suzanna would now be in safe hands for a mantle of professionalism seemed to descend on Harry at the mention of possible sickness — his initial shock at the news was replaced by calm assurance. "Yes, make some tea, Sophia, and some for your aunt. She's in her room. I'll look after your mother."

When she returned to the drawing-room they were both seated by the empty fireplace. He had drawn the curtains and removed Suzanna's coat which lay in an ugly heap on the sofa. She looked a little more herself, but dreadfully thin in a loose-fitting fawn dress, bowed down by her huge, hideous hat. Sophia wondered how she could wear such dreary clothes.

At Sophia's entrance, Suzanna sat up and smiled brightly, a gesture which caused Sophia a sharp thrill of pain. Were they such strangers that her mother must correct her posture and expression in this way?

"Your mother's come all the way from Switzerland. She's been doing great work there," Harry Callwood said.

"What exactly, mother?"

Suzanna looked nervously at her daughter. After all,

Sophia thought, I have no right to ask, she has received nothing but indifference from me.

"Mostly for the women and children, poor things. So much needs to be done. There were so many refugees." She gripped the arms of her chair as if suddenly determined to get up and return to work.

Harry placed a tea cup in her hands. "Now, you are hungry, I expect. Your daughter here has become quite an expert in the kitchen over the past few weeks. What shall she make for you?"

"Oh nothing, nothing. I've done nothing but eat. You know what journeys are like!"

"Some eggs! We have lovely fresh eggs," Sophia said stupidly. It seemed imperative to feed this fragile creature.

But the idea of food seemed to sicken her.

"You go and make up a bed in Helen's room," Harry suggested to Sophia. "That used to be your room didn't it, Suzanna? You'll be able to have a good sleep there."

"Oh no no no, I came to help. I came to look after Mrs Bubb. She used to be very good to us when we were children, she was so kind to me. I thought I must come and lend a hand to make her better."

"Mrs Bubb died this morning," he told her, "so we'll all be glad of an uninterrupted night's sleep."

"I told you, mother," Sophia said reproachfully, "don't you remember?"

"Don't you think she's grown like her father, Harry?" Suzanna asked suddenly. "Yes, definitely. Nicholas always took after me. I went to France, you know, to see where he died. But I couldn't find the exact place. It was raining."

Sophia went to Helen's room and made the bed; opened the window to admit the night air; tiptoed out to the garden and gathered a few roses to place on the dressing-table. She heard her uncle go to his room to talk to Margaret; together they went down to the drawing-room and closed the door.

Sophia was selfishly, bitterly disappointed. Her mother had become a symbol of possible redemption for her; during the last weeks she had conceived vague plans of reconciliation. She would try to embrace some of her mother's causes and perhaps find a niche for herself, although she had hitherto little interest in any of her campaigns. But she had imagined being welcomed into her mother's fold and proudly presented to her world. But it had become painfully clear, even from those brief moments in the drawing-room, that Suzanna was in some ways a refugee herself, with all her strength and passion subdued. There remained only a kind of hectic desire not to be a nuisance.

Sophia went into the kitchen, prepared a tray with cheese, fruit and cake, and carried it into the drawing-room, but even as she opened the door she recognised the hopelessness of this activity, for her mother was lying back in the chair, sobbing helplessly.

Margaret and Harry took her up to bed.

Sophia tidied the room and sat down to eat the supper, a ritual she could not afterwards understand.

Later Harry came.

"Is she very sick?" Sophia asked.

"It's hard to say. We'll be able to tell more in the morning. She'll sleep now. So should you." He led her to the foot of the stairs where she kissed him and went slowly up to bed.

20

HELEN TURNED UP the next morning wearing a surprisingly smart blue dress and navy hat — her glasses winked in the sunlight as she stood in the porch. The prodigal was returned. Margaret's pleasure and nervous deference were painful to watch, though Sophia reflected ruefully that she could scarcely reproach her cousin for lack of filial concern. Anxious to avoid the endearments and explanations of a Callwood family reunion, Sophia retreated to her mother's room.

Suzanna had slept well and now lay quietly in Helen's narrow bed, her gaze on the open window through which she could see the cheerful wind-puffed clouds. She looked very peaceful, being unaware of the ordeal which Harry had initiated for her by contacting Simon Theobald.

"He must know that she is here and in a poor state of health," he had told Sophia firmly. "He has a duty to support her and a right to be told where she is."

"But, uncle, she won't see him. And if she did he'd frighten her and make her even more unhappy."

"I won't suggest he comes here. No — and I certainly wouldn't let him see her if I thought he wouldn't be gentle with her."

But when informed by telephone that Suzanna was in Needlewick, Theobald had said that he would cancel all his engagements and motor down immediately.

Sophia was amazed by this prompt concern. She was also distressed and frightened. She remembered the last time she had seen them together — Nicholas's funeral. She had watched them carefully, hoping for reconciliation in this moment of shared grief. She had seen their eyes meet once, and Suzanna start towards him with extended hands. He'd waited until she was very close before turning away.

Sophia took an action she would not otherwise have considered: she telephoned Colin and asked him to accompany her father. "He won't understand the state she's in," she told Colin desperately. "I just don't know what will happen when they meet. She will have us to protect her, but what about him?" Colin replied calmly that he would try to ensure that her father did not come to Needlewick alone and added that he was convinced the meeting would be very civilised.

When she had replaced the receiver, Sophia found that her hands were shaking and her heart pounding. Why had she involved Colin? What had she brought on herself?

Her mother seemed pleased to see her. When Suzanna smiled the years melted away from her — her teeth were a little discoloured, her skin had lost its gloss and her eyes their brightness, but the shape and enchantment of her smile were the same. She wanted to know the cause of the commotion downstairs, but lost interest when she heard Helen had arrived. "I don't think I've ever met her, have I? Perhaps at Nicholas's service. I don't remember. Wasn't she a rather plain little thing?"

"Very clever. She's been very successful at the university."

"Yes, it's odd, isn't it – I used to think my children

would shine and poor Margaret's daughter would have no hope, confined to Needlewick like I had been. But Nicholas died. Oh, I never stop thinking of him, never. I see him all torn apart, his head broken. He would have been such a great man, a kind man, not like your father."

The tears fell down her cheeks into her ears.

Seeking to distract her, Sophia blurted out: "Uncle Harry telephoned father this morning and told him you were here. He said he'd come and see you."

Suzanna did not seem troubled by this news after all.

"It'll be all right now I'm here," she said. "I'll be all right. Anyway, I'd like to see him, there's so much I need to discuss with him. We should have talked about your future much more carefully — and Nicholas's. If I'd had my way Nicholas would never have gone. It wasn't worth it, it wasn't worth it, they should have listened to me."

Sophia dabbed at her face with a handkerchief.

"Nicholas had to go to the war, mother, he was the right age. They needed him."

"They didn't need him. My lovely boy! I loved him all those years and they gave him to German guns. It needn't have happened. They needn't have fought like that."

"But, mother, there had to be a war."

"No, Sophia, no." But she could not sustain her anger or her train of thought for long. She turned her head away. "They wouldn't listen to us. They wouldn't listen. But we were the women who gave birth to those boys for them. It costs a man nothing but a moment's pleasure to bring a child into the world. That's why life is so cheap to them. They don't pay and pay, body and soul."

"Please, mother, don't get too upset. Please. Nicholas would hate you to cry for him like this."

"Don't say that, Sophia, don't say it! I asked too much

of Nicholas — I always expected him to understand. He took too much on himself when he was only a child. Surely I can cry for him?"

"Oh mother, I let you down so badly," Sophia said bleakly, forgetting that Suzanna was ill and could give no comfort.

"You are your father's daughter, Sophia. You didn't let me down. You did exactly as I did. I chose your father. So did you."

"I couldn't understand you. I never knew how Nicholas did but he always seemed to understand."

"My lovely boy," she cried, turning her head from side to side on the pillow. Then she recovered and took Sophia's hand. "But I tell you what, Sophia, no-one can blame us for what we did. I won't let anyone reproach you."

"What do you mean?"

"Neither of us had been taught to think at all. I had to have the truth hammered into me day by day, blow by blow, violently, because I didn't know how to learn. So I made so many mistakes and even now, sometimes, I forget everything and want only to come back here to Needlewick. I'm so tired."

"Will you go home to father?"

"Never, never, never to your father."

She was very quiet for some moments, but at last she turned back towards the window and said softly: "I met him here, you know."

"Yes."

"I thought, when I first knew him, that he would feel as I did about Needlewick. I used to take him everywhere; I showed him all my favourite places. I thought he would share it all. He seemed so delighted. He was irresistible, Sophia. Well, you know that."

Yes, Sophia knew his charm and power.

"But he took me away from Needlewick." She looked

—197—

at Sophia directly, as if for the first time. "Sophia, we should have insisted on your receiving a proper education. It was so short-sighted. But I thought your looks and money would be enough. And you seemed bright." She began to cry again, and said weakly, over and over again, "I wish you could have gone to a proper school. You should have gone to school."

Sophia stroked her hair, soothed her and encouraged her to sleep. She felt exhausted by her mother's emotion and helpless disappointment. Finally she murmured: "It's not too late, mother. I'm not that old, I could still go to college."

"No, no, you'll marry the man your father found you. You'll marry him and do as I did."

"But I told you I'm not engaged to him any more. Anyway, he's a good man."

She was not listening, "He's titled, isn't he? That would please your father."

"Colin is a good man. He's been very generous to me."

"That's what I thought about your father when he piled presents into my lap. Everything I could wish for, even the Tunnel Woods, he bought me the Tunnel Woods, as if that could ever bring them back to me."

Sophia wiped her face and smoothed her hair. "But you've led a good life, think of all those people you've helped. Father didn't take that away from you. Look at all you've done for those hungry people in Germany."

But Suzanna was no longer listening.

In the end Sophia had to call for her uncle, ashamed of having provoked such distress.

Sophia found it strange to be in Roundstones with Helen again, and, despite herself, was amused to find that she now regarded Helen as the intruder, the disturber of the status quo. Suzanna had made little impact, sad and sick as she was — Roundstones seemed to have extended warm, comforting arms to her and enclosed her effortlessly within its old walls. But Helen, who asked nothing at all, set the family on its best behaviour and jarred the rhythm of the household. At lunch-time Sophia fancied that she could hear her mentally drumming her fingers on the table at the tedium of the conversation. When it came to clearing the dishes between courses it was Sophia who leapt up to wait on Helen, fearful of incurring her irritation by involving her in the mundanities of life. The only topic that really attracted anything more than her polite attention was that of Suzanna.

"Do you think I might go up and see her after lunch?" she asked. "Just to introduce myself. I don't remember her at all, and I've always so admired her."

"I suppose it can't do any harm, she seems a little calmer now," her father replied, "but she's really not at all well, you know, you must not excite her in any way."

"I have a letter to post," Sophia told Helen diffidently. "I wondered if you'd come to the village with me later."

"Yes, if you like." Her indifference to Sophia was all the more galling because it was so clearly unaffected.

After lunch Helen disappeared upstairs while Susan and Sophia washed up. Prior to Helen's arrival Sophia had not resented her domestic chores or her necessary subjection to Susan's unrewarding company, but now she felt ready to stamp on the tea towel in rage at her cousin's indolence and thoughtlessness.

"It's a good job I'm here," she told Susan, "otherwise you and poor Mrs Callwood would be terribly overworked. I don't think Helen is used to domestic life — she's got a very senior position at the university, you know." Susan shrugged and slammed more crockery into the sink.

Later, when Sophia went upstairs, her mother's door was closed. Behind it she could hear quiet womens' voices.

By the time she and Helen left the house the sky had darkened and rain threatened.

"It looks as if we'll have to walk quite quickly," Sophia observed. "Are you sure you want to come? It may rain."

"Oh yes, I don't get enough exercise these days, I'm sure."

Conversation was very difficult. Helen had little interest in small talk and made Sophia feel silly when she tried to ask questions about her work. Sophia wished she could make some learned, mathematical pronouncement which might impress, or at least provoke discussion, but she was unable to produce anything.

"How long will you stay?" she asked tentatively.

"Lord knows. I don't expect I'll be able to stick it for long. Perhaps until mother is ready to manage with that new Makepeace girl."

It struck Sophia that Helen would be of little use in helping her mother over this difficult transition.

"Susan has made remarkable progress over the last few weeks," she remarked.

"What about you? It's good of you to have stayed on so long. I expect you'll be wanting to go home."

"I'll see what my father says. He'll be here soon. I'll obviously have to take care of mother."

"Oh, I wouldn't worry. My mother seems quite happy to have adopted another invalid."

Her words contained no malice, yet Sophia felt dismissed, both from Needlewick and Suzanna's life.

"You went to see her."

"Yes, we had quite a little chat. She seemed all right, I thought."

They were nearing the village.

"The place gets smaller every time I come back!" Helen said. They stood for a moment on the bridge at the foot of the High Street while she cast an unsentimental eye about her. "The Makepeace place seems to be a little smarter."

"You used to go there often, didn't you? I remember feeling such a grand lady when I visited Mrs Makepeace with you."

"I suppose I did too, really. Shall we go in and say hello?"

"Oh no, I don't think so. I mean it's years since I was there. I've no reason to. You can if you like."

She shook her head, relieved, and hurried past the door.

"I'd like to call on Mr Gresham, though," Sophia told her. "He's been very kind to me since I've been here."

"I wonder how you've put up with Needlewick, I really do. I couldn't, for any length of time."

"Your mother seemed to need me."

"Yes, there'll never be anyone like Mrs Bubb again. Poor soul!"

"Why do you say that?"

"She never had any life of her own, did she?"

"Don't you think so? She must have been happy at Roundstones. She seemed to have made herself part of it."

"She was part of everything," Helen replied sharply. "Every part of my childhood. Every time I went out, or came in, Mrs Bubb was there. She seemed to understand me and know when I had had a sad day or a happy time."

Sophia wondered why Helen had not rewarded such devotion by at least visiting Mrs Bubb during her last illness. Indeed Helen must have felt the need to justify this neglect for she added: "I suppose I resented Mrs Bubb for knowing so much about me."

They walked on in silence until they neared The Grey House; Sophia was afraid of shattering the intimacy of Helen's last remark.

The sun suddenly emerged and shone hotly on the wall — they could smell the mortar. "I hate it now Eleanor's dead," Helen murmured.

Mr Gresham was clearly alarmed by their arrival, though he must have heard their approach for he was standing at the French windows, neither in nor out of the house.

"We won't disturb you!" Sophia called. "Helen's here, and we've just been to the post office and thought we'd call in case you were in."

He took Helen's hand. It had been a mistake to come, Sophia could tell, but she had been unable to resist this legitimate opportunity to visit him. He was rumpled, as if from sleep, and Sophia suddenly realised that perhaps a social call must seem cruel after the delicacy of their last encounter.

"The garden looks as lovely as ever," Helen said. Sophia thought that perhaps she was too short-sighted to see how overgrown it was, how the weeds grew in the flowerbeds and the borders needed a trim.

"I do my best," Mr Gresham responded.

"I'll come and give you a hand with it," Helen offered suddenly. "I expect I'll be here for some days — until mother is settled with the new maid."

He thanked her dutifully but seemed more alarmed than comforted by this suggestion.

They next spoke of Suzanna. He regretted that he had taken no action over the letter, which would have at least warned the Callwoods of her intentions. "We are both at fault," Sophia told him, "I said nothing either. It seemed so unlikely somehow that she would actually come."

After a pause she added: "I've come partly to say good

—202—

bye in case I don't get another chance. I expect I'll be leaving within the next couple of days." No such plan had been formalised until that moment — it was his garden that had convinced her that she had no further cause to stay in Needlewick. Mrs Gresham's garden no longer, it was a tangled, autumnal muddle of plants she had not seen or tended. And Sophia could do nothing to assist Mr Gresham, who stood so uncertainly on the small terrace — she could not offer to put his garden in order for him. "So, if I don't see you again, goodbye, and thank you."

They set off back down the brick path where dandelions had pushed themselves up between the stones.

He called after Sophia: "Did you ever get to the Tunnel Woods, then?"

She turned, very conscious of Helen, "No, I never did. No. Goodbye, Mr Gresham."

"He ought to move away," Helen pronounced when they were at a safe distance from The Grey House. "It's all too much for him now she's gone."

"I don't think he could bear to leave Needlewick, do you?"

"Don't be silly. Of course he could. It's foolish to brood on old memories of the past."

Later Sophia said: "Helen, my mother's in your room. Would you like me to put an extra bed in the guest room — or what? I've been wondering where you might sleep."

"Oh don't bother, I'll sleep on a sofa tonight. As soon as they move the body I'll use Mrs Bubb's room. I've always liked the view from there."

They could not pass Middlecote hall without calling. Word would certainly have reached the family there of the new arrivals at Roundstones and of course of Mrs Bubb's death. It would be an unforgivable slight not to go in.

They were shown into the drawing-room where the sisters were at tea. Lady Middlecote at once leapt to her feet. "My dear Helen, what a surprise! My dear girl! And Sophia!" They were embraced, ushered to the table and plied with tea and cake; attentions which had an unfortunate effect on Helen who withdrew into herself like an irritated sea anenome.

"And how is Cambridge?" asked Lady Middlecote.

Helen regarded her coldly. "I'm not sure what you mean. My research is progressing well, thank you, especially as most of the students are on vacation. I still find the city an enjoyable place to live."

"Your mother will be so pleased to see you. She misses you dreadfully, I know," floundered poor Lady Middlecote.

"I think she's been rather occupied with Mrs Bubb," interjected Sophia gently, "and you know my mother has turned up?"

"Yes." Mrs Parditer suddenly reached out and took her hand. "How is your mother?"

"Very nervy, very unwell. Exhausted, I think. I'm afraid we are both rather a burden on poor Aunt Margaret at present."

"Don't be silly, Sophia. She's probably delighted Suzanna's here. I told you that." Helen clearly had no time for conventional apologies and courtesies.

"And now my father is likely to appear at any moment," Sophia added, "and I'm afraid I'm rather dreading it."

Mrs Parditer's interest, if possible, quickened. "You think he'll come?"

"He's legally responsible for her, you see, so my uncle felt he should be told." Sophia recognised that at last she had found someone who would comprehend her fears. "I don't think Uncle Harry quite understands what my mother has endured, or how furious father was when she left. It won't be a happy meeting."

Helen shifted uncomfortably in her ungiving, upright chair. "We've just called on Mr Gresham. He looks as if he's come to terms with his loss."

Nobody quite knew how to respond to this remark.

After the cousins had gone Lady Middlecote sighed. "I feel very cut off from them all. From Margaret and Suzanna in particular. I don't feel I can help them at all."

"It's natural you should feel it now that Suzanna is back. Our experience is so divergent, we have nothing left to share, except memory — and some memories would be wisest forgotten."

"It's all so acute when one is young. All the love and pain and excitement. Don't you think? I should love to feel something of that intensity again."

Deborah was sitting very still as her gaze followed the now-distant figures of the young women who had crossed the footbridge and begun the ascent to Round-stones. Nothing's changed, she reflected, we two were always on the edge of the dramas, as we are now. I doubt if Suzanna has ever lost her intensity.

21

As SOPHIA LAID her hand on the brass latch of the garden door at Roundstones she knew that she had reached a turning point; once inside she would be sucked into the whirlwind the arrival of Colin and her father would undoubtedly cause. Pulling down that stiff metal latch was one of the few actions in her life that she recognised as significant. And then the door was open, and there was no time for reflection.

Colin was standing on the lawn with Aunt Margaret, waiting for her.

When she approached to take his proffered hand, she could feel the warmth of his body though they did not kiss. His solidity was somehow a surprise after weeks during which she had been able to remember only the way his hair had become ruffled one particular evening, or the sound of his voice saying an inconsequential phrase. Decide, decide, she thought in a panic, even as she was smiling and welcoming him, whether you love him or not. You must decide.

They were left alone. Her father was already closeted with Uncle Harry, now Margaret ushered away Helen to see about supper. They soon had only the flowerbeds for company. Sophia thankfully recognised that, although the fresh wind and scudding clouds did not offer comfort, they might provide a welcome distraction. She took his arm, and with the other hand held down her skirts, or pushed back long strands of hair which had been fretted loose in the now considerable gusts of wind.

He did not seem nervous, but looked about him with interest, telling her that she had written so much about Roundstones he could not fail to be curious on this second visit. He added that her father had seemed quite composed on the journey, although he had welcomed Colin as a travelling companion. They would both stay the night in Cheltenham, and had already booked rooms. Sophia was warmed by his air of competence and normality; she had become so enmeshed in the small domestic dramas at Roundstones that his coming seemed to fling open the door of the outside world. She began to wonder whether the question of their future together would after all be raised immediately; she hoped not, she was so nearly sure, but not quite, not quite.

But it became obvious that he was simply awaiting the right moment to speak, for he paused, took her hand which had been resting on his arm and turned her to face him.

"I'm glad you telephoned me, Sophia, because I've been looking for an opportunity to speak to you again. I know that this is a particularly difficult time for you, and I do not want to add to your troubles, but yet I must speak."

She had no premonition of what was to come; her mind was engaged only on what she would say; what would be her answer now. She did not therefore see the pain in his eyes, or attempt to interpret the sudden tightening of his fingers on hers.

"I've come to ask you to end our engagement completely," he said.

She was so astonished that at first she could say

nothing. She thought stupidly, It is I who was doubtful, not him.

Then she said, without thinking: "Does my father know this?"

They had walked to the part of the garden furthest from the house; an observer might have wondered at their sudden absorption in runner beans.

He did not attempt to conceal his hurt or his contempt at her response but replied at last: "As a matter of fact, yes."

"I'm sorry. That was a foolish question. It's not what I wanted to say. I'm sorry." She was very near tears — suddenly to have the choice wrenched away from her; the safety net which she had once made a feeble attempt to abandon but had actually retained to give her courage was now to be taken away then.

Colin's voice, unusually sober, continued: "I think we both knew that once there was talk of postponement there could be no going back. One ought not to be ambivalent about whether or not to marry someone, I think."

"No."

"I have felt the strain of indecision. I want to be free of you completely. I can't go on like this."

She could not resist asking: "Is there someone else then?"

They had wandered on and were now by the garden door. He leant upon it, and the sun, making a brief appearance through a sudden torn gap in the clouds, shone full on him.

"You still don't understand how much I loved you, do you? Or you wouldn't ask that. I just won't subject myself to any more pain."

She went to him and laid her head against him, so that her cheek was turned to the warmth of the sun. He did not push her away but made no move to embrace her.

"What if I've changed my mind?" she murmured.

He seemed to flinch. "No, it's too late."

"I wrote. You wrote so often."

"Yes. And I searched each one of your letters for a sign of affection, regret, and found none. And then I gave up looking. You sounded lonely, so I replied."

She gave a great indrawn gasping sob: "Oh God, I wish I knew how to love you."

Then he did put his hand up to her shoulder. She could hear the smile in his voice. "You do little for my self-esteem."

They moved apart and continued their slow progress.

"Shall you stay on here much longer?" he asked.

"No. I don't really belong here. There isn't anything for me to do. And it's such a small world, hidden away. But I'll have to see what happens about my mother."

"Of course."

"I wish you could meet her."

He laughed. "I fear she would be too much for a simple soul like me."

Before re-entering the house they solemnly shook hands.

"I do wish you every happiness, Sophia," he said.

"Doesn't that sound straightforward?" she replied, smiling, but she scarcely knew how to release his hand, and could not bear to follow him inside.

Simon Theobald had arranged to dine at Roundstones. By the time Sophia was sufficiently composed to meet him, Colin had left so she was at least spared the embarrassment of confronting them together. She was waiting for her father when he finally emerged from Harry's study, but was completely unprepared for the way he took her in his arms and embraced her. When she put her hands on his back she could feel his rigid spine through the soft cloth of his jacket. I cannot be forgiven this easily, she thought, or has anxiety for my mother at last softened him?

At dinner he was at his most genial and brought to the quiet Roundstones dining-table a polish and wit its conversation generally lacked. He listened with absorbed interest to Margaret's nervous chatter, asked Helen informed questions about her work and seemed quite able to discuss rural affairs with Harry though Sophia knew, from a remark he had once made, that he found the doctor's company tedious. Sophia said little, avoided his eye, but watched his charm work its familiar magic. Helen removed her spectacles and smoothed her hair, the most self-conscious gestures Sophia had seen her make, and Margaret, despite herself, soon glowed and giggled.

At first Sophia too was seduced by the excitement he generated. All her life she had worked to achieve his goodwill — his approval, or more usually the absence of his disapproval had been enough to give direction to her day. If he kissed her, or smiled, or said: "What a becoming frock, Sophia," she would retire to bed happy, and wallow in the memory of the moment. Her weeks in Needlewick had allowed her to escape this distortion; she was able to live and evaluate and experience more freely though she could not of course completely shed his overbearing influence. But now that he was again physically present she found herself seeking her reflection in the hall mirror, handling her cutlery more fastidiously, and smoothing her voice for him. Her heart jolted when he smiled at her; when he addressed her she stumbled over her reply.

But then she began to wonder at his presence in the house where his wife lay sick in body and mind through years of struggle — years in which he had turned his back on her. When catching his eye Sophia suddenly recoiled at the knowledge that he had so recently attempted to manipulate her future by his rigid outrage at her uncertain engagement, and she sought to armour herself against his allure which threatened to melt her again into the pliable clay he could fire and glaze according to his fancy.

Beyond an enquiry into Suzanna's well-being and a grave nod when Harry responded that she was still sleeping, he did not mention her until after the meal. Neither man showed any desire to be left together so the entire family trooped into the drawing-room where Theobald remarked: "A delicious dinner, Margaret. I'm sorry to have intruded on you this evening, but I feel so anxious about my wife I could not return to Cheltenham after all. I can no longer leave you to bear the responsibility for both my wife and my daughter."

"Oh they're no trouble, no trouble at all! Dear Sophia has been such a help with poor Mrs Bubb. And Suzanna, I was so pleased to see Suzanna!"

"Yes, but Harry seemed to suggest that it will be some time before she recovers, and I cannot leave her here indefinitely."

Sophia intervened with as much composure as she could muster: "My mother must surely decide her own future, father." She felt that he was taking possession of Suzanna as if she were a trunk of clothes or an old piece of furniture to be shunted about at his pleasure.

He smiled at her. "Of course. If she is fit to decide for herself. Harry?"

"As I told your father earlier, Sophia, I have asked another doctor to call tomorrow — a colleague with some expertise in cases of nervous disorder. But she seems happy here for the time being."

"I'll go up and see her now," Simon Theobald stated.

"No." Harry spoke firmly. "She must rest. She is asleep, and should not be woken."

"Well, I would like to look in on her, in any case." Simon Theobald rose to his feet and Sophia realised helplessly that there was no stopping him, her uncle was no match for such strength of will. "I'll come with you. If she's asleep we'll leave her," she said, trembling with outrage and anxiety.

She led him up the stairs and softly opened the bedroom door. Inside, the room was dim for the twilight paled the floral curtains only slightly. Suzanna was curled childishly on her side, a plait of hair fallen across her face, but there was nothing childish in the way her fist was clenched on the pillow, the thumb caught under the fingers.

They stood at the door for a moment watching her, then he went over to the window and drew back a curtain.

"We'll leave her," Sophia whispered, "as she's sleeping."

But he beckoned her over to him. "I wondered when you thought of coming home?"

"Probably with you, when you go."

"I've missed you."

"I'm sure the house has run smoothly without me."

"It's not the same without you."

"You seemed resigned enough to my marriage to Colin. I would have had to leave home then."

"Yes. I wanted to apologise to you. I behaved badly. It was a disappointment. I wanted to see my little girl happy."

"I believe Colin will have told you that there is now no question of our marrying."

"Yes. I was very sorry, but of course I understand."

His conciliatory, sympathetic tones were so unexpected that she came near to taking his hand or even allowing tears to fall. Instead she said bravely: "I thought I might enrol at college in London and gain some qualifications. I wondered about perhaps renting my own accommodation."

Both knew she had no money of her own.

He asked, inevitably: "What qualifications?"

"I'm not yet clear what is available. I thought of nursing, or perhaps learning to type."

This was a mistake. The predictable, obvious, yet contrasting nature of these two options betrayed the insubstantiality of her plans. Indeed, the suggestions had fallen off her tongue from nowhere, she had not thought of them before. But they were at Roundstones, in the twilight, and his apology still hung between them. She felt that this was her only chance.

"Very well then. I suggest you come home and we'll talk and make arrangements, perhaps for next year as I expect you're a little late to enrol for this autumn's courses."

Sophia recognised that the first obstacle was being flung in her path. She raised her head and looked down to the river, now only a dull ribbon in the gloom. "We'll see," she replied.

They had woken Suzanna; when Sophia turned back to the dark room she could see that her eyes were open. She touched her father's hand and he went and sat by the bed.

"Suzanna, I came to see how you were."

"I'm very well, thank you, Simon."

He reached for her hand but she plucked at his fingers to tear them away. He stroked her hair. "My dear girl," he whispered. "My dear girl."

She began to weep.

"Make him go away, Sophia, make him go away. Why is he here?"

"Suzanna," he murmured, "Suzanna, my dear love. Wouldn't you like to come home to me?" He clasped her hand in his, and kissed it.

Suzanna, too weak to resist, gazed past him to Sophia. "Please. Please. Please, Sophia!"

"Father, she's too distressed. Come away." Sophia had never seen him display such emotion, yet she could not

—213—

trust him. He was a man who could plan every word he spoke, every tear he shed. "Father!"

She took his arm and led him out on to the landing, though she sensed his anger at not being left alone with Suzanna.

Stupidly, in an attempt to comfort him, she said: "She was telling me about how you met her near the Tunnel Woods."

"God, the Tunnel Woods!" His hand was on the newel post. He turned to Sophia and his eyes were very blue and cold. "I hope no-one told her I sold them a few weeks ago. She would be most upset to know they will be cut down and the land ploughed."

Harry was waiting in the drawing-room. He seemed to have gained courage during their absence, for he spoke firmly: "Perhaps you'd like to come back tomorrow afternoon? Then we'll have a clearer idea about Suzanna's condition." He held Theobald's hat. "I'm sorry we can't put you up here, but I expect you'll find somewhere locally or you could take the cab on to Cheltenham. I took the liberty of ordering it for you." He held the door open. "Goodbye, Simon, until tomorrow afternoon then."

Sophia stood on the stairs and watched her father adjust his hat. Then the door was closed behind him and Harry turned to her.

"I think you were right, Sophia. I should not have telephoned him. He should not have come."

22

SOPHIA DID NOT sleep for several hours. Her brain teemed with memories of the day; faces, words, swam in and out of her mind and then she would come to herself and think wearily, Oh, I'm still not asleep then.

Small wonder I'm overwrought, she reflected, my fate has been sealed today; I won't marry Colin, but instead go to college and become a typist. I will wear cheap shoes and a black skirt and take trams from one dirty area of London to another.

Her room in Roundstones offered no comfort for it was a harbour she must leave within twenty-four hours and a reminder that from it she had achieved nothing, discovered nothing. Now she would never reach the clearing in the Tunnel Woods. The diaries, stored carefully in the bottom of her case, rebuked her. They had seemed to offer her a future, a new direction, but all they had done was unleash unhappy demons from the past. And following her to Needlewick had come first her mother, then Colin and her father — all in their various ways to disturb the habitual tranquillity of Roundstones. And everything that had happened had been blundering and unintentional. She had made several blind attempts to reach the clearing, released dangerous, festering emotion in Michael and perhaps even destroyed the fragile calm that Mr Gresham had restored to his life.

But at last she slept, dreamlessly and deeply, to be awoken at seven by an unusual bustle in the passage outside her room: cries and questions, hurried footsteps, Margaret's voice.

Sophia went to the door and called: "What is it?"

Helen was outside in her nightgown, standing at the top of the stairs.

"Your mother has disappeared."

"No! How do you know? What do you mean? I thought Uncle Harry had given her some drug to make her sleep."

"It must have worn off."

"Where have they looked? She can't be far."

"Sophia." Helen took her by the arm. "She had a photograph — I don't knew where she got it. There were two girls."

"Yes, I know, perhaps Aunt Margaret gave it to her. It was in Mrs Bubb's room — it was taken in the garden here."

"No, it wasn't the garden."

"What then? Helen?"

"It was the clearing in the Tunnel Woods."

Helen had lost her habitual calm demeanour and was agitated, embarrassed, irritated by the drama of the situation.

"I think she's gone there."

"But she's so weak. It's so far. She can't have gone all that way!"

"Yes, but I think she has. I think she'll be there. Will you come with me?"

*

A wicked wind had got up in the night and it must have rained towards dawn for the grass was very wet. Sophia was ill-equipped for an early morning walk against a robust autumnal wind — her wardrobe at Roundstones contained only light frocks, a couple of cardigans and a jacket. But Helen walked doggedly, her head well down, dressed in a thick skirt and heavy woollen jersey which she had borrowed from her father. The river was muddy and fast moving, carrying no reflections, only its own silt. Leaves skipped in their path, whipped from the trees by this first wind of winter.

"What do your parents think, then?" Sophia asked breathlessly. "Do they feel you might be right?"

"They said it was worth a try. Father's gone to the village, he thinks she'll be there, or at the Greshams, or the church. Mother can think only of the funeral."

"But Mrs Bubb is dead!" Sophia cried.

"Yes, but what could mother do?" Helen seemed to understand her cousin's resentful exasperation but made no attempt to soothe her. "I hope Suzanna hasn't gone far. None of her clothes is missing, only her nightgown and an old bathrobe of mother's."

"What about shoes."

"Her shoes were there."

The wind knocked the strength from Sophia but she was forced to do little running steps to keep up with Helen. Her legs were soon wet to the knee, her feet soaked. After a while she said to Helen: "It's nice of you to bother!"

"Of course I bother. I feel responsible. When I called in to see her last night she showed me that photograph and it took me by surprise. I said: 'Good Lord, the clearing!' and she seemed terribly excited and said: 'Yes, yes, I thought you'd know.'"

"But, Helen, it was father who upset her by arriving so suddenly."

"She said he was going to cut down the Tunnel Woods. Was she right? I thought she was talking wildly."

"But how did she know? He mentioned it only after we'd left her room."

But Suzanna must have overheard. Was that what Simon had intended?

Soon Sophia was so warm that the wind on her neck was a relief, though strands of hair caught in her eyes and mouth. She reached out and took her cousin's arm. "Helen, you do remember the Tunnel Woods, then? I thought you must have made yourself forget."

"No, I hadn't forgotten. Not entirely."

"What was there, Helen, tell me?"

Helen walked faster, her arm unyielding under Sophia's hand.

"Good Lord, nothing! A child's fancies."

"But my mother was there, too. Why would she want to go back?"

"I don't know!"

"Helen, who was in the photograph? I couldn't make it out."

"No, I couldn't, either. I thought at first. . . . but of course I was wrong."

"What did you think? What Helen?"

She suddenly stopped.

"I'm sure she's there. She must be there. We should have brought some other people. If she's ill, we won't be able to get her back. She'll be cold and exhausted."

"Won't your father think to bring some men from the village?"

"Yes, but he may be a long time. We could at least have brought a blanket or something."

Sophia realised that Helen was right; they were completely unprepared. She had followed Helen more in the realisation that this was her only chance to find the clearing again than in the expectation of finding her mother

—218—

there. But, if they did find Suzanna, they would have nothing to offer her, no hot drink, no dry clothes, not even the promise that help would come soon.

Sophia had a stitch in her side but hurried on, doubled up, stumbling over rocks and roots in the path. The Tunnel Woods seemed to retreat.

By the time they reached the fence, rain was falling in cold, strong shafts. It soaked through their clothes and on to their backs and necks. Helen stood still at last, rain streaming down her face.

"Helen!" Sophia shouted. "Helen! I know a way. Helen, this way!"

But Helen would not move. "Who built this?"

'I don't know! My father probably. I don't know. But I know a way, up here."

"Sophia, she won't have been able to get through! She won't have been able to find another way!"

"She might! She might!" Sophia knew they must go to the clearing now. She pulled Helen away, and plunged through the undergrowth until she found the break in the fence.

Among the trees the rain had as yet made little impact, but soon great drops would begin to fall from the treacherous canopy of leaves. The woods were very still under the blowing, sighing tree-tops, as if tensed for the penetration of the rain. Now Helen led the way again. She marched purposefully towards the Tunnels, not faltering when a thorn caught at the back of her hand or rain fell from her hair into her eyes.

At the Tunnels she stretched out her hand to Sophia. "Come on. Hurry!"

The Tunnel was still and thick with stagnant darkness.

The cold of the rain was nothing to the chill of the Tunnels. Sophia thought her only link with life was Helen's warm hand and the cuff of her wet jersey — she could smell the damp wool. But in minutes they were clear.

Helen turned without hesitation to clamber up the steep rocky bank between the Tunnels, though the rocks were wet and slippery. At the top she extended her hand to Sophia and dragged her up before turning to find the path through the bracken.

But, of course, there was no path. The bracken was now a dense forest reaching to their adult shoulders and beyond, and the path Helen had beaten with daily use had long since disappeared.

Panic and frustration welled through Sophia's knees, thighs and stomach.

"Helen, you must remember!"

"But don't you see? There's no point even in trying. Your mother can't have come this way. The bracken would be trodden down."

"Helen, she might be there. Wasn't there another path? Helen!" Sophia was shouting at her. They must get to the clearing. They were so near. Helen must not give up now.

Helen plunged into the bracken, thrusting it aside with her hands, stamping with her feet. She did not hold the heavy fronds aside and they slashed back in Sophia's face. Their legs were grazed where the sinewy stems resisted them. Soon they were submerged in the rancid bracken, head-high as Sophia remembered it, but with no alluring little path to ease their way.

But they came to the clearing.

Suddenly the bracken began to thin and they were in an open space.

"She's not here," Helen said.

Nothing was there but a small clearing in the woods, with a hawthorn tree in the middle, and grass flattened by the rain.

"What will we do, then?"

Helen gazed at the tree.

"You'll have to stay here. She might come. She might be in the woods. I'll go and look for her."

"You'll get lost."

"No, I won't."

"Helen, let me come with you."

"No, you must wait here. This is where she'll try to come."

"Wouldn't you rather stay?"

"No. No. I'll look for her. You stay."

She seemed afraid, as was Sophia, of being left in this dripping heart of the woods. There was no opposing her.

Helen made her way round the edge of the clearing and disappeared among the trees.

So Sophia had reached her grail. But she had missed the enchantment before and could not find it now, for through her adult eyes the clearing was small and unremarkable. The tree was perhaps rather larger than average and certainly very old, its leaves already tinged with the sad yellowing of autumn. It never used to rain here, Sophia thought angrily, looking to the sky for relief, but the clouds were thick and relentless, not a shred of blue.

She walked to the tree, seeking shelter. It did seem a little drier there for the leaves underfoot were not shiny with wet like the grass; when she reached down and picked up a handful they felt damp but warm. She crouched against the trunk and drew her inadequate jacket about her. She was very cold, and very disappointed, and suddenly felt foolish. Her poor sick mother could not have staggered a few yards, let alone all these miles. Sophia knew that she should have acknowledged this earlier, but as usual her judgement had been flawed.

She leaned her head back against the trunk which felt wonderfully solid compared to the swaying pliable green stalks of the bracken, the flattened grasses, the steel shafts of rain. Her body's crouched stillness after such a rush of activity made her faint and very tired. She closed her eyes, listening to the rain on the leaves, the wind gusting over the tree.

A man would come with an axe, the weapon would gleam as the blade caught the sun, and he'd swing back his strong right arm and cut at the tree. And, after a hundred such swings of the axe, the tree would whimper and fall with a great sighing compression of leaves and branches, and the heart of the clearing would be broken. And he'd bring out his saw and his knife and hack at the branches until the tree was a neat pile of logs with no life of its own, a pile of logs like any other pile. And the soft grass would be strewn with fragments and chippings and twigs and shavings, and the dead leaves would be hidden by piles of green leaves which had minutes before been swaying and living.

Perhaps wheat would grow here, or a house be built with neat bright gardens and modern plumbing, pipes reaching into the soil which had nourished the tree, or a road would cover the earth and mens' feet and mens' machines would stamp on the hard stones.

And what of Helen's people? Were they waiting by the tree for Sophia to go, ignorant of the brutality that was planned for them?

Sophia opened her eyes and stared into the pool of leaves.

Here was an end to her quest, waiting for her after all, singing to her as the wind in the leaves, as the bird on the branch. I absolve you from dependency, the rain sang. I absolve you from being a victim of your mother's dreams or your father's ambition. I absolve you from your passive, shared culpability for your brother's death and your malicious destruction of your cousin's child-

hood. Knowing this, from now on, you have only yourself to blame.

She was alone in the clearing. The rain fell on the
leaves.

"Sophia. Sophia. We've found her. Sophia!"

She was almost too cold to move, indeed by moving
she sacrificed her last fragments of warmth — the contact of her back with the tree, her knees with her body.
But Helen was waiting on the edge of the clearing, her
straight hair a helmet in the rain, her clothes clinging to
her stout body.

Together they ran from the clearing. Helen did not
want to linger there. Sophia understood and did not look
back.

They were following the old path through the woods,
the elusive, short-cut route which Helen seemed to
have found without difficulty — it, at least, was not
overgrown.

"Where is she then?"

"Michael's with her. He found her. She couldn't get
into the woods, of course, because the path by the river
was blocked. He made some shelter for her. He's gone for
help. She's in a terrible state, Sophia. She'd been trying
to force her way through the fence."

Suzanna was lying in a sheltered hollow near the path
where bracken had been hurriedly beaten down and
where a thick, dense undergrowth formed a rough tent
for her. A man's jacket was spread round her shoulders
and Helen's woollen jersey across her feet. Her hair lay
in thin fair strands on the earth.

Her hands were bleeding.

Sophia knelt by her mother's side and took her head
into her lap. Suzanna did not stir.

"That wicked fence!" Sophia cried. "She would have

—223—

been all right. She just wanted to go to the clearing."

"That place! I'm glad she didn't."

"No, you mustn't say that, Helen. It was my father's fence that did this to her. She must have loved the woods so much. It was my father. He's always been in her way." She held the still, cold figure more closely. "Mother, you'll get better! I'll look after you. I'll bring you back here and we'll come to the woods and the clearing where it's so peaceful. We'll find what you were searching for. I'll look after you. I'll earn money and we'll work together. I'll look after you."

"They're coming," Helen said.

They had brought blankets and a stretcher for Suzanna. They laid her gently down and covered her face. Sophia stumbled behind with Helen as they walked back along the top of the valley, leaving the Tunnel Woods, age old, nestling in the valley, impervious, vulnerable.

23

TWO OF US dead in one year, Deborah Parditer thought. How terrible it is to bury friends, for in a way they anchor us to life. Even Suzanna had been a constant. Though she had been, at times, elusive and cruel, life was less safe without her.

But it had been far easier to mourn Eleanor properly; Deborah could weep for her pain, and for the empty rooms and gardens at The Grey House where letters and callers had always found welcome, understanding and friendship. But Suzanna, dead, stirred in Deborah the same mix of feelings as she had when alive, with the result that Deborah could feel very little grief for Suzanna. Rather, she was relieved that her friend's restless, demanding spirit was at last at peace; that Deborah need no longer fear that word of Suzanna would suddenly come to disrupt and intrude on her settled, comfortable existence; that she need not worry that Suzanna would turn up, dainty and elegant, however ill-clothed, to make her feel clumsy, heavy, over-dressed. For even when very sick Suzanna had contrived to create discord in Deborah's staunch heart by returning late at night, too distraught to see her friends, leaving

Deborah to fret and ask herself over and over again: How can she be too ill to see those who love her? It had taken all Deborah's considerable will-power to fight down the old feeling of resentful exclusion and make excuses to herself for Suzanna: She's very sick, she's very tired. Now, at last, that yearning to be loved by Suzanna could be laid to rest, at last there was no point in measuring herself up against Suzanna, who was dead and could reject no-one.

Surveying the company assembled in Needlewick churchyard, Deborah wondered how many shared this ambivalence towards Suzanna's memory. Certainly Simon Theobald, who stood straight and still, as he had throughout the service, and whose face betrayed no sign of emotion.

Meanwhile, beside Deborah, Jane wept unashamedly and held George's arm for support. Jane's love for Suzanna had always been much more straightforward, Deborah thought, not far from complete admiration. Jane had regarded Suzanna as a being from another, unattainable world and therefore never attempted to emulate or equal her.

Margaret, by contrast, seemed very composed. Indeed, for one who had lost a faithful servant and a sister in the space of a week she looked positively jaunty. Good heavens! Wasn't that a brand new hat? She certainly hadn't worn it to Mrs Bubb's funeral — what a ridiculous little cockade poked out of the brim — and surely her skirt was shorter than usual by at least an inch. She seems less anxious than I ever remember her, Deborah thought, her brow is relaxed. What has done this? Is it because Suzanna is dead, because at last Margaret does not have to live in her sister's shadow? Deborah almost cried out at the sudden knowledge that she never saw Margaret without comparing her with Suzanna, even when Suzanna was far away. When she looked at Margaret she always thought: It would be so exciting if Suzanna were here; or: Of course, Suzanna was the lovely one, Suzanna was the most gifted sister. Poor Margaret, we never allowed her to flourish, Deborah acknowledged, we expected her to be over-shadowed. Only Harry, who now stood at his wife's elbow, had truly recognised her worth and loved, cherished and respected her all these years, and for her sake tolerated the ripples Suzanna's great storms had inevitably sent flowing out even to Needlewick.

Unexpectedly, Harry raised his eyes and his gaze caught Deborah's. How much he understands, she thought. Dear Harry. But, as they moved from the graveside, it was John Gresham who sought her out and offered his arm. Poor John, who had just seen another fragment of his wife's life committed to the earth, yet who had enough self-forgetfulness to recognise Deborah's loneliness and come to her side.

At the churchyard gate, Deborah turned for one last look. Everyone had left except Sophia. Throughout the ceremony, she had stood at a little distance from the rest of the family, her face calm, her hands firmly clasped together. Now, even as Deborah started towards Sophia, Helen went up and touched her cousin's arm. Immediately Sophia put her hand to her eyes, as if her tears had been awaiting permission to fall.

As she and Helen at last walked slowly away, Sophia was struck by how time had elapsed so that the days between that wet morning when she and Helen had brought Suzanna home, and this day of Suzanna's burial in the loamy Needlewick soil, had passed as if she'd been in a sleep, disturbed frequently by busy dreams and brief awakenings. She remembered wishing that the slow march along the top of the valley, with one hand in

Helen's, and the other steadying her mother's bier, might never end. There had been a dogged purposefulness about that walk, a calm, a unity which she knew would be shattered the moment the front door of Roundstones was opened to admit them. And sure enough, time since then had been fragmented into sorrowful conversations, packing, preparing, weeping, with no truth, no reality to any of it.

Suzanna, even in death, had thrown Roundstones into disarray. Where should she lie? At last Harry's study was cleared, and she was placed amidst the dark furniture and heavy medical volumes in the one room she must rarely have frequented. Sophia was intimidated as much by the room as by the body within and could not at first bear to visit her mother there. But she went once with Margaret to stand by the slight, white figure with its delicate hands.

"Do you think she was ever happy?" Sophia whispered. "I don't think I ever knew her when she was really happy."

"Why yes, Suzanna was always happy. At least, as a little girl, she usually got what she wanted." They suddenly smiled at each other, recognising the fatuity of this remark. Then Margaret said: "The trouble with Suzanna was that she could never learn to forget herself. She had so many passions — she followed them all, sometimes ruthlessly, but she always left a little bit of herself behind, could not give the most important part."

"Why? Why was that?"

"She never knew," Margaret replied strangely. "Oh, she was always trying to find something which would release that in her."

"What about the clearing?"

"Oh yes, the clearing. There was an answer there."

"What did she find? Aunt?"

Margaret made a small, impatient gesture with her

hand. "My dear girl, Suzanna always knew what she wanted from the Tunnel Woods. Everyone who goes there knows what they are looking for. And do find."

"And you?"

"Oh I was like many younger sisters. I wanted only Suzanna's love." She reached out and straightened a fold of her sister's gown. "Do you know, Sophia, it is a terrible admission to make to you, of all people, but I feel happier for her today than I did on the day she married your father."

Margaret went to a shelf and tucked a book into line with its neighbour, twitched a drooping white bloom in a vase on the mantel and moved to the door. "Come along, Sophia, we've got so much to do. Susan Makepeace is still so slow."

In the evening, Sophia took a last walk to Needlewick. All along the lane she looked for Michael. She had to thank him for not bearing a grudge from daughter to mother. But there was no sign of him, and perhaps, she reflected harshly, she did not deserve the comfort that expressing her gratitude to him might have offered.

On the way up the High Street she passed the Makepeace cottage, and remembered her mother's words about the village still being poor. Is it poor? she thought, I haven't noticed. She had never looked beyond the uneven fronts of the cottages and was too preoccupied to pay attention to them now. She found her mother's newly covered grave and stood there a while, shivering under the grey sky and the fierce westerly wind that brushed through the old yew tree and blew faded petals and leaves from the rose bushes along the churchyard wall. The only sign of Suzanna was a neat rectangular strip of soil. Sophia crouched down and laid her hand on the cool, crumbly earth. I wish I could at least be sure that I loved you, she thought. But in any case, I won't forget what I said to you, mother. I found the clearing. I understand. I won't forget.

She moved on towards The Grey House. She thought afterwards that Mr Gresham must have been expecting her for when he showed her in to the drawing-room she saw that a fire had been lit there and glasses and a decanter set out on a table by the window.

"Thank you for coming to the funeral," she said at once, anxious that the ostensible reason for her visit should be clearly stated from the first. "We all appreciated it, for your wife's sake as well as your own. It can't have been easy, another funeral in the same churchyard."

"How are you now, Sophia?" he asked, ignoring her references to his own state of mind.

"I'm all right, I suppose, though I feel a little lost. Everyone's leaving tonight or tomorrow. Actually, Mr Gresham, that's one of the reasons I came to you. I'm hiding from all the bustle. I need a retreat. I hope you don't mind. Everyone's going off with a fixed purpose, except me."

He led her to a chair and poured her a glass of sherry and they sat together at the window watching the weakest leaves from the apple tree skate across the grass.

"I'm to drive home with my father and Colin in the morning," she continued at last. "I think the journey will be all right, although as I expect you've heard there is now nothing between Colin and me at all."

"Do you mind?"

"I feel bruised, of course, but only, I suspect, because in the end it was he who decided it, not me." She smiled a little ruefully.

"So what will you do, Sophia?"

"Well, I think now I will go to Zurich after all, to see

the people my mother was with, and then I suppose I must find a means of earning my keep, since I have no wish to be dependent on my father longer than necessary."

"How is your father?"

"I don't know. I never know. Disappointed, I suppose, more than anything. I mean, I suppose we've all let him down in our different ways."

The room, when she fell silent, was so quiet that the little china clock on the mantelpiece sounded intrusive; both were very aware of the time passing.

Sophia's heart was beating fast, she was afraid she would not have time after all to complete her mission. She looked across at Mr Gresham to give herself courage and found that his gaze, as always full of tenderness, was for once fully on her, not, as was more usual, a little averted as if fearful of actual engagement.

"Actually I also came to thank you," she said at last, "for everything you've done for me. You've been so kind. I didn't know you before this summer, I didn't remember what you were like, I suppose I was too young. And I wanted you to know, because it seems so sad and pointless that you shouldn't, that I love you. Oh don't worry, I expect nothing, ask nothing, just that you should know."

She had not stopped to question, when planning this visit, what his reaction would be. She had only felt that it was imperative that he should know. It was all she had to give him. He sat very still in his chair, and then carefully replaced his glass on the tray at his side, stood, held out his hand to her and led her out of the French windows and along the stone path to the gate. There he took her in his arms and rested his cheek on her hair.

"You know that you are precious to me, Sophia," he said.

*

After she had gone John Gresham returned slowly to the house. Once, near his wife's favourite apple tree, he stopped, laid his hand on the trunk and laughed. He remembered sitting on the bench with Sophia earlier in the summer, the diary between them. It had been a moment of light for him to see her there in Eleanor's garden, perhaps because she was his last charge on Eleanor's behalf and afterwards he might rest, perhaps because she had glowed with health and youth, and, unhappy as she was then, he could not be untouched by the latent vitality in her.

He laughed again as he re-entered the house and picked up her glass. He held it to his lips and drank what she had abandoned. The realisation that he was lovable, however transiently, gave him an instant of pure joy; he had been asked, for once, nothing, but given much.

Finally he moved into his cold study and took the photograph from his desk. It was a little dusty, he polished it with his sleeve. His wife gazed at him from amidst the stiff folds of her veil. You were right after all to leave me so little to remember you by, he told her, I won't find you in this empty house, or the garden, or even among your things. But you're in her a little, and in Helen. And did you, he demanded suddenly, ask her to come to Needlewick partly for my sake? Did you, Eleanor?

But there could be no reply, nor had he time to linger in search of one. He returned to the drawing-room for the tray and went off to look for clean glasses. Deborah Parditer had said she'd call. He sighed. She had mentioned that he should take a holiday. She would expect him to make plans.

Sophia took the field path to Roundstones, the memory of his kiss lending a lightness to her step. The sky was overcast; in a strong gust of wind a fine drizzle fell. The ground floor of Middlecote Hall was already lit, as was Roundstones across the valley.

At the footbridge she performed one last rite: she removed the diary from her pocket and held it over the rail. It cost her no pang to drop it into the fast-flowing, opaque water. The exercise books floated along bravely, untroubled by the imminence of their complete immersion. With little patches of darker red appearing on the thin covers, they sailed out of sight.

"Very well, Mrs Gresham," she said, "I'll hide no more in safe places."